To; my

MW01073398

DOOK#L.

SHOWDOWN AT SCATTER CREEK

God Bless!

John T. Wayne

John T. Wayne

The Dukes Grander

4-29-18.

THE GASLIGHT BOYS (series)

THE NEW STANDARD IN WESTERN FOLKLORE!

SHOWDOWN AT SCATTER CREEK

John T. Wayne

THE GASLIGHT BOYS (series)

THE NEW STANDARD IN WESTERN FOLKLORE!

Mockingbird Lane PRess

Showdown at Scatter Creek
Copyright © 2016 John T. Wayne

Mockingbird Lane Press—Maynard, Arkansas

ISBN: 978-1-944541-77-4

Library of Congress Control Number: 2016937156

0 9 8 7 6 5 4 3 2 1

www.mockingbirdlanepress.com
Graphic art cover: Jamie Johnson

This book is for my father Billy Gene who never knew his real father was John Wayne, "dad," this one is for you!

If a man refuses to follow God's law, what on God's green earth makes you think he will follow a manmade law?

John T. Wayne

THE GASLIGHT BOYS

From 1861 – 1865 a storm rolled through our nation and in its wake left behind a path of death and destruction. Over 100,000 children lost everything they had come to know including both parents. This tragedy took place during the Civil War and sadly for years after; during a period known as Reconstruction. What became of those children? How were they instrumental in shaping the future of our society? These questions are answered in my series of books called, "The Gaslight Boys." Charles Dickens is credited with being the original Gaslight Boy, but there were many other Gaslight Children created by the war. The Gaslight Boys series brings to life the hardships, the conditions and individual struggles buried and /or forgotten by time.

These are the stories of the young men and women who grew up to become great in their own right, men and women of the great society. Some of them became great, some became outlaws, and some died short of the chance. The Gaslight Boy novels are their stories.

John T. Wayne

Authors Note:

I have seen the name Captain Nathaniel Bowlin spelled a few different ways, the same with Sheriff Wright, but in order to honor my colleagues at the Green County Genealogical society we will use the oldest and most common spellings in the archives. A special thank you to all of the helpful members of the Greene County genealogical society for their assistance with this book, in hopes that our heritage is richer than any of us might have ever perceived.

Court Documents of Greene County Arkansas dated 1874

Concerning the killing of Sheriff Wright.

Editor's *Gazette*:

As so much has and will be said about the unfortunate difficulty which occurred here on the 13th ult. in which Morris W. Wright our late sheriff, lost his life, and as the surviving principle actor in the occurrence has been long known to many of your readers, and as many conflicting accounts have been given of the affray, I send you a brief but unbiased statement in the matter, in justice to the living and the dead. I was an eye-witness to the combat, and familiar with all of the parties and the differences which led to the fight.

A writ was placed in the hands of Wright (the sheriff), for the arrest of Jesse Bowlin and Zack Holmes, his brother-in-law. Jesse Bowlin is the brother to Captain Nathaniel Bowlin. The two were charged with breaking open a store and stealing a lot of goods there from. Wright proceeded to the home of Captain Nathaniel Bowlin, with a large posse of men, to make an arrest. The captain was not at home. The accused were both present and made resistance. A fight ensued in which two of Wright's men were killed. Holmes and Jesse Bowlin broke to run when they were fired upon and Jesse Bowlin was shot down while running. The posse came up while he was lying in a helpless condition, supposed to be mortally wounded and Wright's men shot him in the head, as was carried out by order from Sheriff Wright. Some witness accounts indicate the body of Jesse was then hung from a nearby tree.

Captain Bowlin returned home to find his brother murdered, while Holmes had made good his escape. However, prior to his return Wright and his men had thus entered the home of Captain Nathaniel Bowlin and took all of his guns, spices and anything else of value. This aroused Captain Bowlin and resulted in a deadly hostility between Bowlin and Wright which carried through to the end of the Civil War. Captain Nathaniel Bowlin then charged that Sheriff Wright had laid an ambush for him and his men with Bowlin's own weapons, but the ambush was noticed beforehand by one of Bowlin's riders and thus avoided. Friends of the captain then interfered and forced Sheriff Wright to return the weapons to the Confederate Captain, but he denied removing anything else from Captain Bowlin's residence at that time.

By this time Sheriff Wright had on many occasion used his fire arms upon men when he could have avoided such action altogether. On several occasions Wright and his posse had killed the residents of Greene County until he had become a terror to every living citizen. He had become reckless, dangerous and unscrupulous. The conduct of Wright just before his death became so strange that everyone in Green County began to sleep with a gun under their pillow or carry a gun at the ready for no one knew what his temper would be on a given day. During this time repeated threats on the part of Wright to kill Captain Bowlin had been communicated to the captain.

On the 13th of April G.S. McNabb came to Gainesville armed. He was brother-in-law to Sheriff Wright. Most everyone was coming to town to pay their taxes now that the war was over and the Federals had won, and so it was no surprise when Nathaniel Bowlin arrived in town. As Bowlin entered the post office Wright was coming out. With nothing short of a curse from Sheriff Wright the two men dragged iron and began shooting at one another. Wright was killed and before Bowlin could reload G.S. McNabb unleashed his weaponry and began to fire on the captain from behind. He wounded the captain, but that was all and Bowlin made good his escape. Bowlin returned home and sent word that he would come to town and surrender to the authorities as soon as his wounds would permit, which course was advised by his friends and legal-council. McNabb took his sister, gathered all of her belongings, Sheriff Wright's savings and left town. It was later learned that they had headed for California with $30,000 of the county's money.

* *

It is important to note here that virtually all the land we know today as farm land was once virgin forest. Green for as far as the eye could see. Over the last 150 years the farmers have cleared the flatland on either side of Crowley's Ridge to produce capable crop growing topography which yields gainful crops year after year. This was no easy task and took decades to accomplish, but at the time my story takes place, the flat land about

Crowley's Ridge was still timberland, just as most of the land on Crowley's Ridge still is today.

Chapter 1

Trouble has a nasty way of determining for a man what he does during the day. Along with such a thought I struggled with my saddle, having lugged it the better part of three miles. Noting a nearby fallen log, I made my way over to it and dropped my saddle, bridle and blanket roll to relieve my arms. I had just caught a whiff of wood smoke as I was about to cross the line into Arkansas from Missouri by way of the St. Francis River. I was in boot-heel country or just leaving it if you prefer, three days out of grub, out of coffee and my horse had gone lame a few hours back. I wasn't much to look at, just a boney kid of five feet eight inches tall, but I could hold my own and prided myself on doing just that when things turned rotten, which of late was more often than I cared to admit.

Wood smoke was a welcome sign in this part of the country, but such a signal could just as well be a bunch of soldier boys and I didn't want any truck with them at the moment. Every time I found myself at a soldier fire of late they were trying to get me to join one side of the war or the other. Fact is, I was trying to get as far away from the Civil War as I possibly could. Not that I was a coward, I just didn't think I had lived yet. At fifteen I was trying my dead level best to keep the hair on my head.

My canteen was empty, my saddle was way too heavy and I was buckling under the load so when I smelled the woodsmoke I dropped all of my gear and sniffed the air for a few minutes. It took a moment to discern what

1

direction the smoke was coming from, but eventually my snout told me it was from the south. I have a pretty good sniffer and to date my nose had not let me down. Only problem is trouble doesn't offer up any detecting odor in advance of its arrival.

I didn't know of any Yankee outfits this far south so I shucked the rest of my gear, all but my pistol, rifle, and canteen then headed in the direction of the camp. I had been walking along what is now called Crowley's ridge. Skylining myself on a low part of the ridge overlooking the St. Francis River, I looked over the vast sweep of county to the east. It was a swamp infested forest for as far as the eye could see.

The smoke was there, lifting straight up into the prevailing breeze then drifting along the ridge in my direction. I could see their camp from where I stood and the site was a makeshift affair, disorganized and ramshackle. It didn't give me much hope, but if I could get a meal and fill my canteen in the river, I would not want anything else.

There was a steep ledge I had to get down, but I was game and in no time I was walking along Crowley's Ridge, although down in the bottoms. They had some horses tied, and if the unknown party had an extra I was going to see if I couldn't borrow one and go back for my gear.

There were two men and a boy about my age around the fire. They had coffee, but I also smelled catfish frying in the pan, just retrieved from the St. Francis River. The fish wasn't a little one they had caught either, it was filleted into several strips hanging over a tree branch while only one piece at a time would fit into the fry pan.

"Howdy," I said startling them.

2

It was plain as daylight they hadn't been expecting anybody. I wasn't really anybody to fret about, but you would have thought the law had just dropped into Ol' Dooley's Lodge to make an arrest.

"Where did you come from," the oldest among them wanted to know.

It seemed to me I was staring at three rattlers ready to strike at a moment's notice, but I did the kid thing and shrugged my shoulders. "I came down off the ridge. Y'all must not be from these parts." I myself wasn't thirty miles from my original homestead, the one Pa had worked until he turned up missing a few years ago. I knew everybody in this part of the country, but I didn't know these fellows.

"Well, you're here, you might as well join us," the elder man said.

He was a rough looking man with gray hair and a square set jawbone. His face was dirty, his nose had met with someone's fist one time or another and never got straightened. He wore a pale color hat lined with sweat and dirt.

He was leaned back against his saddle waiting for the fish to fry and he didn't pay any more attention to me. He went right back to whittling on a stick, his mustache twitching this way and that as he carved up more imperfect lines on his piece of wood.

I glanced at their horses and they were good, too good for this bunch, but then I had seen some real low down folks sporting good horses. I stepped closer thinking to get a look at the brand they wore.

"My saddle is back up on the ridge, I left it lying on a log about a mile back. I'd be obliged if I could borrow one of your horses and go get it."

"Help yourself, just make sure you bring the horse back," the old man insisted.

"Yes sir, I'll be sure and come straight back. I'd like to share some of that catfish if you don't mind another mouth."

"There's plenty," he observed paying more attention to his woodcarving than to me.

I hadn't gotten around to looking at the brands, but something about the horse I stepped up on seemed almighty familiar. If I had looked first, I would have never jumped on the back of that horse. I took off bareback and headed up the trail. It wasn't easy coming down and I knew it wouldn't be easy to lead a horse back up, but if I jumped down and led him I could do it.

When I got close to the log where I'd left my saddle I brought up short. Captain Franklyn Starr was sitting there with his boys staring at my loose saddle and gear.

"Now I wonder who..." he started to say.

"Pa look, its Duke John Robinson and he's got Ol' Sho-me!"

"Well, I knew about the Starr family and I knew about Ol' Sho-me, but I hadn't seen the horse in nearly three years. When I heard the accusation I immediately recognized the horse I was leading. Like an old man receiving a death bed conversion ten seconds before he entered the gates of hell, I dropped those reins like they were on fire and dove back down the hillside, a steep hillside which no man in his right mind would dive down, but a boy in his youth wanting to live?

"Careful or you'll kill the horse," I heard Captain Starr admonish.

Gunshots rang out behind me. I didn't look around to see who in the family was pulling the trigger. I heard bullets whiz by my head and bounce off trees. Suddenly I was falling headlong through the bramble and the brush on the side of Crowley's Ridge and then I hit hard. My head bounced off a log along with my right shoulder and when I staggered to my feet, I fell backward over the same log and landed in a heap. I heard them coming but, I was in no shape to run, not now. The only thought running through my mind seemed to be I was about to be hung for stealing a horse I had no part in stealing. Chances were those fellows back at the camp were saddled up and riding away by now. They would have heard the gunfire and commotion up on the ridge.

I blacked out. I landed so hard I gave myself a concussion, but in the springtime foliage I had left no visible trail. The family hunting me didn't know where to look, and when I came to I was surrounded by darkness. I lay still for a long time to make sure I was alone. The last thing I wanted to do was stand up to a gun stuck in my ribs.

Bubba Starr had always had it in for me, even when we attended school together at Gainesville, so it was no surprise he would want to hang me for stealing a horse, even though I hadn't stolen it.

Gainesville was the only settlement in Greene County at the time the Civil War began. The Sheriff was Maurice Wright, pronounced Morris, and he was quite a character. He was the type who wouldn't take much guff off anyone. If he arrested someone for being a horse thief they hung lickety-split. Suddenly, my worry was that he would catch

wind of my escapade and dispense justice before he gathered all the facts.

My problem now seemed two-fold. I couldn't go home. I had burned the house after Pa was presumed dead because I didn't want any settlers moving into the empty cabin. Pa had buried a lot of money on the old place, but unless you knew it a body would never go digging there. If someone moved into the place while I was away, I would have a big problem getting the money out of the ground once I returned home. It seemed to me the only way to ensure I didn't have such a problem was to burn down the house.

My other problem had been my brother and sisters. They had been a good deal younger than me, all of them ten or under. I had left them with a good family in Greene County, but only with the understanding that they would find good homes for them. If they had done so or not, I had no way of knowing. I had been wondering the country the last few years trying to grow up without getting myself killed. That wasn't easy with the entire country at war. If all had gone well, my siblings would be a bit older now, maybe even able to think for themselves, but there was no way for me to know the truth of the matter.

I started to sit up and hit my head on the log once more. In the dark I couldn't see the fact that somehow I had landed under the log. This had no doubt saved me from capture. I had known the Starr family for a long time and they were a family that wouldn't do anything if they couldn't do it from the back of a horse.

Chances were they had taken my gear. They had not been the best of neighbors even when Pa was alive. I had been gone two, almost three years now and I wouldn't be

welcome to return home. My trip to St. Louis had found the conditions in the city less than desirable. The war was still raging up and down the Mississippi and I just wanted to be left alone so I could grow up. That wasn't happening though.

I had been kidnapped by Ol' Slantface and the preacher while strolling along the streets of St. Louis. Without the help of Captain Grimes I would have been sold into slavery and me a white boy.[1] Once the boys and I escaped, a change of plans was in order. I decided to head home, dig up Pa's money and ride west. I had heard of the orphans being hired by the ranchers out west and I was an orphan, so I figured they could hire one more. The fact orphans from the war were being called cowboys didn't bother me none at all. I wanted a job. The name cowboy was derogatory, but a boy like me doesn't much care what he's called as long as he eats regular.

After resting my head a mite, I slid out from under that old log and stood up. In the dark I couldn't see a thing. I have to admit, I was scared right down to the soles of my feet. I didn't know what to do. It would be too risky for me to go home now, yet I needed Pa's money. If I was seen by anyone, I could be strung up for horse stealing and you know what, I didn't even have the dad-blamed horse anymore.

Once I headed west I didn't plan on ever coming back to these parts. Once I had the loot all dug up it was in me to ride as far west as a boy could go, somewhere such as California or Oregon. I wanted as far away from this silly war as I could get before something else happened.

---

1 Ol' Slantface-Mockingbird Lane Press 2014

I sat down on the log and rubbed the side of my head where it hurt. My skull was swollen and out of shape. My neck was throbbing and I didn't know whether I could climb the hillside again, but I needed to see if my saddle was still there.

I hadn't any truck with the Starr family, not once I got into a fight with Bubba Starr a few years back. My fist had broken his nose and he never got over it. He and a couple of his friends had jumped me after school one day and it didn't quite work out the way they had figured. There were three of them and I whooped them all that day, picked up my school books and headed home.

Pa whipped me for getting into the fight, but I took my licking and proudly bore the brunt of it. Now Pa was never a mean man, but he had been a hard man and there's a difference. He hadn't allowed much time for child's play, and looking back, I'm glad he handled me like he'd done. I would never have been able to survive the last few years had he not been stern with me way back then.

There had been more than one lonely night since he'd disappeared where his oldest boy wished he could see his pa one more time to tell him thank you for everything, but that was just a childish dream. I'd likely never get the chance. My father was gone for good; the only thing missing was a body to bury. I don't guess Pa was the first man to ever die and never be dug a grave.

He had left the house that day three years ago while we kids went off to school. I have five brothers and sisters. That evening our father never returned home. The next day I looked all over the countryside for him, but there was no sign. The neighbors had not seen him, no one had spoken with him and he was nowhere to be found. The

one thing that had always stuck in my head was that Franklyn Starr was missing those days too. Captain Starr had returned eventually, but Pa never did.

With no parents at home we hung on for three weeks thinking Pa would return when he was able, but he never turned up. That had been a year before the Civil War and then it was clear something had happened to our father. Since our mother had been gone for some time, I took my brother and four sisters into Gainesville to find a place for them to stay and I headed for St. Louis, but before I left I burned down our house in the De'Laplaine Swamp down. My younger brothers and sisters had no need to live in the house, for they would be cared for by other folks who had a home, so burning the place had been my only logical choice. If I ever returned home to find the house occupied, there would have been a devil of a fight retrieving Pa's money what was buried in mason jars all about the place.

I had always helped Pa, for my younger brother and sisters were not old enough to understand the hardship we were facing, but Pa had always insisted I should know. In that way, if something ever happened to him I would have an idea what to do.

Well, now here we were in that exact situation. What had caused Pa's demise? There was no way to hold the family together once Pa was out of the picture, because he was the only authority those brat's I call siblings would listen to. I had a dickens of a time just getting them to town.

Where they had finally settled I had no idea. I had left to be on my own, to see some country and learn the tools I would need to survive. This was no easy task, for I no

longer had an instructor like my father, no one willing to guide me. I was on my own and I knew it.

I had grand ideas in those days of how a boy should be able to grow up, how he could make his own way and hold his head up. Now after nearly three years of struggling to survive along with thousands of other orphans created by the war I was no longer so sure of myself.

I thought back to the days of my innocence and I knew I would never see them again. No child should have to grow up as I was doing, but I knew deep down I was not the only one. Orphans were being created daily by the Civil War. I bumped into them all of the time. There simply was no getting away from it. They had a right to survive, if they could. I had the same right, and let me tell you, it wasn't much when characters like Ol' Slantface and Jeremiah Culpepper could kidnap and sell you into slavery at the drop of a hat. I had gotten free from him and the preacher, but what had I gotten myself free to do? I was now considered a horse thief by the Starr family.

Chapter 2

I was sitting on my log thinking when the sky turned gray in the east. I had to dig up Pa's money. I couldn't go west without it. I also needed a new horse. Mine had gone lame a few miles back so I'd turned him loose. I didn't have the heart to shoot him like most men were known to do. I wasn't that grown up yet.

To the best of my knowledge he was roaming the ridge up in Missouri somewhere not far from the state line. That was the closest landmark where we had parted ways, so I'd been carrying my saddle forever it seemed, but in reality I hadn't gone all that far. What I didn't know was that dad-blamed horse of mine had been coming right along. He was following me like some lost puppy.

As the sun began to come up in the east I saw my horse out in the bottoms. He was chomping on some green foliage having a fine time at my expense. I wasn't sure if he was laughing at me, but if he wasn't, he should have been. There was no doubt in my mind he had turned up lame. Now here he was following me like he wasn't even hurt.

I studied him for a long ten minutes. He was getting around all right without a rider on his back. Maybe all he had needed was a few days rest. I was no judge of horse flesh, but Jericho was as fine a horse as I was likely to ever get my hands on. So imagine my surprise when I saw him taking liberties with the forest undergrowth. I'd had a

devil of a time letting him go the day before, but turning him loose was something I thought I'd had to do.

When I could see well enough in the shadows of the trees I started to climb the steep hill to see if my gear was still there. I could only take a few steps at a time before stopping. That lump on my head was making any travel difficult. Finally about halfway up the hillside I stopped to rest. My head and shoulder were throbbing.

When I looked back at the horse he was cropping grass in the small meadow he'd found. He wasn't going anywhere in a hurry. He was less than thirty yards from the St. Francis River and he had all the grass he could possibly want. As for me, I was on a three day hunger, or was it four. I could no longer remember. That blow I'd received during my fall had left me unsure of anything. I did find my rifle on the way up the ridge.

As I topped the ridge I could see my saddle was gone. Just as I expected, the Starr family had taken everything I owned. Well, tell me I'm not stupid! I vowed then and there to get my gear back, all of it, even if it killed me. I wasn't going to go anywhere without my own saddle. First of all, it fit Jericho like a glove. Second of all, it was mine.

I picked my way back down the hillside then walked out to the meadow where Jericho was still feeding himself. How lame he was I had no idea, but I needed to ride him a little way at the least. My head was rearranged into some hideous shape I knew I wouldn't recognize if I looked into a mirror, but I hadn't one.

Jericho stopped to look at me when I drew near, then went right back to eating. He knew me, and I was no worry to him. I pulled his head up and looked him in the eye.

"Well partner, it looks like you're all I got," I told him. I stepped up beside him and leapt on his back, but I almost slid off the other side. Normally I could do such with little effort, but like I said my head was messed up something fierce. I grabbed hold of his mane and hung on giving him his head. He knew where I wanted to go and we moseyed off in the direction of home.

A few miles south we waded into the river and crossed with me hanging onto his mane. As we came up the other side I noticed something odd in the distance. It was the two men I had met the day before. They were each hanging from a tree limb. The boy was nowhere to be seen. I studied them for a moment then moved on. No doubt the same awaited me if I was somehow spotted by the Starr family.

Jericho was still a little lame, but nothing like he had been. If I could get him near home I could give him a well needed rest. The place I had in mind was a hole-in-the-wall, a place called Scatter Creek. Nothing much ever went on there, but a fellow could hang out at the creek for a few days and get news from here or there. Someone was always coming down to Scatter Creek to target practice in the woods where nobody would see them wasting ammunition and the sound of gunfire was somewhat contained.

Wasting ammunition was a cardinal sin at the time. With the Civil War at full steam wasting lead didn't set well with folks on either side. I, on the other hand, liked to know I could hit what I was aiming at. Pa had taught me a lot, but I had found it necessary to practice because the shooting iron hadn't come natural to me like it did Pa. Pa had been a wizard with any kind of weapon. That was

the intimidating factor about Pa...he could kill any type of animal with a bow and arrow, a gun or a knife. He even knew how to use a slingshot. I had gotten pretty good with a slingshot myself, but not the other weapons, and so I had done my share of practicing at Scatter Creek.

I nudged Jericho and we headed on down the road for there was nothing I could do for those men not with my head banging between my ears. I kept my eyes open because I knew the Starr bunch was still in the area. So far I had seen no evidence they had gotten the kid and it was my wish they wouldn't. If they caught him it would be just one more hanging. If that boy had any sense at all he would get to another state while the getting was good.

I thought about that and realized maybe the advice I'd give the kid was really good advice for me. It occurred to me at that moment that getting to another state was a fine idea, but my stubborn streak wouldn't let me go. I wanted my saddle, my money, and my gear.

The ground flattened out and the ridge moved away from us, so I turned Jericho to the west because I didn't want to be out in the open that much. I kept looking around, because in the back of my head I knew the Starr's had to come this way to get home as well. Bubba had two younger brothers, Asa and Jupiter. It had been told one time that Bubba's real name was Delta Starr and that's why everybody called him Bubba. It was then I remembered the riverboat *Delta Star,* named for a lady of the night down New Orleans way and I chuckled to myself. At least the old man had a sense of humor.

My hope was that the Starr family was ahead of me. I intended that they should stay that way, but if I wanted

my rigging back, I'd have to take it by surprise. I set about planning just how I might do that.

As I approached Crowley's Ridge and the woods once again, I could hear some commotion up ahead. It appeared they had caught the other horse thief, the young boy about my age. I could tell they were fixing to string him up just like they had done the others so I slid down off Jericho and left him to crop foliage in the undergrowth of the swamp.

When I sighted them, they had a rope around the young man's neck and were just about ready to spank the horse he was sitting on. I saw the terror in his eyes just before he saw me, so I cocked the hammer on that new Springfield of mine about fifty yards out.

The cocking of the hammer on my rifle sounded through the silence of the swamp like an anvil being struck by a sledge. Instinctively the entire party froze. Not one of them had a gun out. I had caught them unaware.

"If you slap that horse, Bubba, I'm going to open a hole in you the size of a tea kettle."

They stared at me. I had the drop on them and there wasn't a whole heaping lot they could do about it. Captain Franklyn Starr and his three sons were known for having their way with folks, but with the onset of war it appeared they were taking liberties which were a stretch, even for them.

"Now, very carefully you cut him down because if that boy hangs even by accident, you're going to get accidently shot," I told him.

Bubba looked over to his pa. "What do I do, Pa?"

"You do like he says. Springfield's are well known for their hair trigger."

Bubba walked up to the boy and began to untie his hands. When they were loose the boy yanked the rope necktie off and sat there looking at me.

"Come over here and get behind me, but don't get between us," I told him.

The scared boy did as instructed. I looked at the situation to determine my next move. I had no intention of letting them ride out of here, not by a coon dogs howl. They were a cantankerous bunch what seemed to want to take out folks less fortunate than themselves. I despised such Neanderthals as the Starr family for they were always trying to keep others from ever gaining ground. If they gave anybody a hand, it was to get them out of the picture. Some folks stay on top by keeping other folks down—that was the Starr family in a nut shell.

"Get down off your horses and leave your guns, rifles and all. Drape your gunbelts over the saddle-horn then walk over to Bubba," I ordered.

They followed their father's lead, but not a one of them liked it. When they finished I told Bubba to shuck his weapon and lay it over the saddle on his horse. Once he was out of the way, I walked over and gathered the reins of each animal, keeping my rifle trained on them the entire time.

"I'll leave your horses and your guns at the ranch. You can have them back when you get home."

"Are you crazy? It's nearly forty miles back to my ranch," the old man protested.

"Yes sir, and I figure in forty miles you might develop a healthy respect for the law. Meaning Captain Starr, the next time you decide to hang someone, you had better be sure they receive a fair trial."

"They were horse thieves, they stole my horses, and you're one as well."

"If you are going to accuse me of stealing your horses, I might as well keep them," I explained.

"What? You wouldn't," the captain shouted back.

"Try me," I challenged. "Mr. Starr I've been having a rough time of it since Pa disappeared, so if you don't think I'll keep them just have at it. Now, am I a horse thief or not?"

"You're making an enemy out of me boy,"

"I've been your enemy for years, only I didn't know it. Now that I'm home, I'm going to set the record straight about a few things. I think it was you killed my pa and if I find out that's true I'm going to hunt you down and kill you back," I told him.

His face went a little pale for a moment then turned blood red, which was all the evidence I needed, but I knew it would never be enough to stand up in a court of law. No one had ever found a body. He backed down a mite once he realized I wasn't going to budge and then said, "I reckon you're no horse thief."

"But Pa!"

"Shut up Bubba, I'll handle this."

I stepped up into the saddle then and handed the boy the reins to two of the horses, keeping my rifle in play the entire time. I turned to face them and added, "Where's my saddle and rigging?"

"We left it on the river bank, figured to come back and get it later."

"You start for home, the horses will be there when you arrive," I said.

There had been three horses in all, but there were now six to escort home, seven when you counted Jericho. I was trailing three with me and when we rode by my horse he fell into step with us. I knew he would because he always liked to be with other horses if they were about.

My gear was at the river like they said and out of respect for the boy I learned was Michael Johns, I helped him bury his father and grandfather.

"They killed them in cold blood," he accused while we were shoveling dirt over them. "They were fixing to kill me too."

"There's a war going on, Michael. I don't reckon there will ever be an investigation into what happened here. Men are left to defend themselves against the evil of the day."

"Well, I want some "get even," before I'm through."

"You be careful. The Starr's are a known family in these parts. Even if you're in the right there'll be questions asked. You be careful, you hear me?"

"I'll be careful."

"Come on, let's head these animals home before they change their minds and accuse us of stealing them again," I advised.

That's what we did. We were two days getting those horses back to the Starr ranch and Michael kept Ol' Sho-me for himself. The ranch foreman, Rufus Van Cleve started to raise a stink, but Michael pulled out his bill of sale for the horse and said, "This horse and two others were purchased fair and square. You tell the old man if he comes after me this time, he'd better bring an army and a coffin, because he's going to be the first one to die."

His statement made me proud. I knew he was hurting because he had just buried two generations of his family, but he was game.

We rode away, two lonely boys wanting nothing more than to be left alone, Duke John Robinson and Michael Johns. We had horses and we had weapons, plus I kept most of the bullets the Starr's had been carrying. We headed east toward Scatter Creek. I wanted to rest up a day or two because my horse wasn't yet ready for a full work load and Scatter Creek was the perfect place for us.

If a man wanted to get the lay of the land in Greene County, it was to Scatter Creek that he went. It had always been so, or at least as long as I could remember. At fifteen, I guess my memory wasn't the longest in the county, but it would have to do. I needed information, for I'd been gone nearly three years. Scatter Creek was the place to get it.

Chapter 3

We ambled up the west side of Crowley's Ridge from the ranch and put the flats behind us. Legend was, at one time the Mississippi River ran on the west side of Crowley's Ridge, then sometime hundreds or thousands of years ago it shifted and now ran to the east side. I didn't have the education to know one way or another, but the legend was probably true.

Scatter Creek was not far from the Starr Ranch, but I wanted to get there, put the word out and sort of get a jump on public opinion. If the local folks knew what was up it wouldn't hurt, and it would create a cloud of suspicion on the Starr family if they tried to implicate us as thieves. Especially since Michael had a bill of sale for Ol' Sho-me.

We wound through the thick brush on the hillside and eventually came to the trail. It wasn't much as paths go, not much more than a game trail, but men had been using it for years to gather at Scatter Creek. Jericho appeared to be doing fine as we rode deeper into the forest on Crowley's Ridge.

There was a mimosa bush here or there stretching toward the sunlight, a few dogwoods dotted the landscape on the surrounding hillsides and a tree carved up to say, Scatter Creek, three miles with an arrow pointing the way. I pulled up, staring at the carving.

This was something new to me. I'd been this way many times, but had never seen the need for a sign

pointing the way. Everybody in these parts knew exactly where Scatter Creek was located. It ambled along the bottoms all the way into Gainesville, the county seat. I studied that carved up tree and wondered what such a sign might mean. Deep down in my gut I had the feeling it wasn't a good thing, but a young man can make a miscalculation from time to time. All I knew was I didn't want to go riding into a situation as bad, or worse than the one I'd just come out of. Maybe I had gotten gun shy when it came to meeting new people, but I had good reason what with everyone trying to kill one another.

I nudged my horse and we rode ahead with Michael bringing up the rear. The day was hot and muggy, but not as hot as the last few days. Traveling in the shade like we were had me relaxing more than I wanted to. We were living in a time when a young man had to guard against the intentions of complete and total strangers. A fellow never knew who might shuck a gun and blow a hole in him or why. It seemed to me there were some awful mixed up characters on the loose since the Civil War began.

Eventually we came to the trace leading into Scatter Creek. When I turned onto it, Michael brought Sho-me alongside as the trail was now wide enough to ride abreast.

Michael stood up in the stirrups, looking around. "We must be getting close."

"We are. This patch of road we're on winds down this hill a good ways into the lowest part of Crowley's Ridge."

"What did you say the place was called?"

"Scatter Creek. It's a notch hidden deep in the forest, but it's no secret, everybody in these parts knows where it

is. Folks come here and camp, shoot or practice with a bow and arrow."

"Scatter Creek, sounds like a good place to find trouble."

"I hope you're wrong about that."

We rode quiet while the forest grew darker. By late afternoon shadows began to envelop the forest and shade darkened into night. No sane human would want to enter such a foreboding forest voluntarily. None of us knew what lurked there, the beast in the night or the devil himself. I wasn't about to enter the darker recesses of the forest to find out either. Such a shenanigan could wait till daylight.

When we reached the creek bed I turned west looking for a likely place to camp. Most of what I saw was dry. There hadn't been much rain of late and the creek wasn't running. I had hoped to find water in a hole somewhere and finally I did. That's how a creek can be, one day it's running with water so deep you can't cross it, the next it's dry. We also found a few fish trapped in the water hole, but we left them alone.

We didn't have much, Michael and me, but we did have our blanket rolls, our saddle bags and a good bait of salt pork. We could put together a fire quick enough and we could eat a good meal before going to bed.

I rode up out of the creek bed into a suitable campsite where someone had left a fire pit for future use. There were also split logs nearby waiting for the next traveler. We got busy gathering kindling and soon we had salt pork in the fry pan. We filled our canteens and let the horses drink their fill from the small brook.

That horse of mine had a habit of dipping his entire face into the water and sucking for all he was worth. I had seen him empty a five gallon water bucket lickedy-split.

Little water remained when the horses were finished. What was left wasn't going to last us much more than a day unless it replenished itself overnight. I hoped underground water would seep in and refresh the pool, as I didn't want to move for a few days. This was where I wanted to spread a little gossip.

Now I know what the Bible says about gossip, but what I wanted to do was get the truth out before that Starr bunch let a falsehood take root in the community. The one thing I knew about truth was this; it would always come to the surface. It might take it a while, but it had a way of being found more often than not. Anybody who doesn't believe that is lying to themselves.

This was a camp which locals and travelers used regularly. I know, because I wasn't much more than that at the present. The fact I was from the area didn't stack up as much of an advantage for me. I don't mean nothing good ever came from northeast Arkansas, I mean that I hadn't been getting the education I needed because there was a war on. I learned a lot of things living on my own while in St. Louis, but a young man could do better than attending school more than three or four hours a week.

When I got too hungry, I would walk up to the gates of Mullanphy Orphanage on the corner of Broadway and Convent street and try to get fed, but in order to get a meal you had to sit through a one hour class whether you wanted to or not. Most of the education I had of today's situation and the hope for tomorrow came directly from the teaching ladies who worked there. If they hadn't been

so good at giving me hope, I might have given up long ago.

"What are your plans, Duke?" Michael asked. "What are you going to do from here?"

Well it was plain and simple. I was going to dig up my father's money and head west, but I wasn't about to share my plans with a practical stranger.

"My home isn't too far from here. In fact it's less than ten miles as the crow flies, but I burned the place down so I can't live there, not now anyway." I shuddered as soon as I said it. My mouth was going to get the best of me.

"Why'd did you burn it down?"

I walked right into that one. The last thing I wanted to do was tell him I had money buried all over the grounds. I wasn't a very trusting person at the moment, but then who could blame me after dealing with the likes of Lucifer Deal and the Starr family?

"I might explain it to you someday, but for now all you need to know is that it was necessary.

"If you say so, but it sure sounds funny to me."

"There was good reason. The best, but you'll have to wait to find out what it is."

The firelight flickered, the leaves of the trees and nearby bushes danced in their shadows. Scatter Creek was eerie come nightfall. As for me, I was used to the idea, but Michael was looking around with worry plastered all over his face.

"It's real quiet here at night most times. Only when a storm rolls through does it get downright vicious," I told him.

"I miss my pa and my grandpa," he said, his voice low.

"I miss my family too, but there's not a thing we can do about it," I said. "Crying won't bring them back."

Suddenly I realized just how much Michael reminded me of me. He lost his family and had no one to turn to. I didn't know if he had brothers and sisters or not, but he was alone just like me.

We went to sleep with a slight breeze drifting through the valley. It wasn't long before I dreamed the silly things boys dream about in the night. I saw a fair-haired girl to spend the rest of my days with. She took care of my every need there for a while, but suddenly she became distracted while babies screamed all around me. Run though I might, I couldn't get away from them.

As far as locations went, we were as far down into Scatter Creek as a soul could get. There just wasn't a lower spot anywhere on Crowley's Ridge. For a man to get here he had to take aim on purpose, so when I heard a horse hoof strike stone in the middle of the night I sat straight up.

All was dark, but I could hear someone coming slowly through the heavy forest underbrush. Every once in a while the horse would step on a stick or tree limb and I could hear it snap, the sound echoing through the night. One fact was as certain as the prevailing darkness; whoever was coming sure wasn't an Indian.

I slid my pistol free of its leather holster and waited, lying right where I was. Anybody coming down here this late at the night was either running from the law or a late night traveler not wanting to be seen, neither case was good in my estimation. I looked over a Jericho and he had both ears up, as did Sho-me. Michael however was sound asleep.

Our fire had died down long ago, but the smell of ashes drifted off into the night. Judging by the fire heap it had to be about two or three in the morning. Not a time for anyone honest to be traveling in such a place. I kept that fact turned face up on my consciousness as the unseen rider continued his approach.

When his horse stepped into the creek bed, the rider pulled up short. I couldn't see him yet, but whomever it was the rider sniffed at the dying embers. He knew someone had arrived ahead of him.

"Come on in," I said. "It's a lousy time to be out riding."

I had Michael's attention, for he jerked upright at my words. There was no answer, so I tried again. "We're friendly, just trying to get some sleep."

The rider came forward with caution and I realized before I saw the animal, it wasn't a horse at all, but a mule. A mule walks different from a horse, and by listening close I could tell the difference.

When the rider came into sight, I shoved my gun back into my holster. It was a girl. I couldn't make out what color clothing she wore, but there was a dress atop that mule or my name wasn't Duke John Robinson. In the darkness, I could see a bonnet and shawl as it swung out when the mule moved. I didn't know where she could possibly be headed, but she was going somewhere.

"I hope I haven't caused you any undue concern," the girl said.

"That remains to be seen," I answered. "What're you doing riding out here this late at night?"

"Some soldiers were fighting in a field near our house so Ma told me to saddle up Dandelion and git. I didn't like

the sound of their cannons and guns going off all day and night, so it didn't take much convincing. She said for me to git on down to Aunt Sophie's place at Peach Orchard."

"Where you riding from?" I asked her.

"Piggott Swamp."

"What's your name?"

"Terri. Terri Moore."

"Well Terri, you done missed Peach Orchard by ten miles. Hop down and we'll make sure you get where you're going."

She slid down and led her mule to water, but he wouldn't drink. I had heard that mules didn't take much water, but here was the proof if ever I needed any.

Finally she tied the mule off near a tree and let it crop grass nearby. Untying her blanket roll from behind her saddle, she spread it out near the fire and in no time she had the saddle off the mule. I had to admit, young though she might be, she was not a crybaby. She came equipped with ready, set, go.

I fell asleep once again as I let thoughts of her run rampant in my head. I hadn't the slightest clue how she would stack up in a pinch, yet I was night dreaming about her like she was the only girl on earth for me. Suddenly the crying babies showed up again and I couldn't get away from them.

When morning came, she was fixing breakfast over a small fire when I opened my eyes. Michael was beside her. I must have overslept because the two of them were all buddy-buddy like they had known one another their entire lives. For the first time in my life I felt jealousy. Michael was where I wanted to be. I shook off my feelings and got up anyway.

"You must be a sound sleeper," Terri said.

"I do like my sleep."

"Well, rub the sleep out of your eyes and fill the coffee pot with water. I've some coffee if you want some."

I grumbled to myself but did as she asked, the whole time wondering if I was going to get my own chance to set up next to her. Something told me I was wasting my time, but then what did I know. I looked over at Jericho while I dipped water from the creek and he seemed ready to move, but I had no intention going anywhere just yet.

I wanted to secure our position in the community and Scatter Creek was the ideal place to do so. I knew folks would be along sooner or later, yet the sooner I could tell our story the better.

I capped the cork on the canteen then walked over and handed it to her. She popped it open and filled the coffee pot with fresh water. "Here," she said, "Fill it again."

I looked at her and wondered just who she was. I knew one thing, she was bossy for a young runny nose little lady. I had no idea how things worked at her house, but she was fixing to get a lesson out here where the woods determined for a man what he did of a day.

I trudged to the creek again and dipped the canteen. I realized the water had replenished itself over night, just as I'd hoped. Slowly I walked back over to the fire and handed the canteen out to her.

"Save it, you'll need it for later," she said.

I stared at her then because I wasn't used to having a girl fry cook telling me what to do. I didn't like it much neither. I didn't care how pretty she was, we were going to have a problem if she kept telling me what to do in my

own camp. You see, that's the problem; what I didn't know about women! It wasn't my own camp anymore and no one had bothered to inform me about such crucial matters.

Terri looked up and said, "Why don't you saddle up the horses, Duke. I'll have breakfast ready by the time you finish."

I didn't argue with her. I dipped my head and turned. Seemed to me the best way to handle things for now was to do like she said, but then I remembered why I was here and stopped in my tracks.

Turning back, I once again tried to address her. "I need to let my horse rest a few days longer. He went lame last week and he's not fully recovered yet."

"I thought you were going to see to it I got to my aunt's house?"

"I am. Just not today."

"What do you mean, not today?"

"It's not life or death is it? If we ride now, I'll have to shoot my horse and he's too good for that."

"I think you're pulling my leg. I think you don't want to take me to Peach Orchard."

"I'm sorry you feel that way, but I can tell you Jericho is lame. Give him a day or two and we'll get you to your aunt's house. I grew up not seven miles from Peach Orchard, I know how to get there from here.

"Besides, someone else may come by at any time and they can take you. I don't necessarily have to be the one you know. Scatter Creek is a gathering place for local folks. Or it used to be."

During our exchange, Michael hadn't said a word, but his eyes swung back and forth between us and a couple times, I thought he might speak up, but he didn't.

Terri looked at me as if she was trying to measure me for courting or for a coffin, I didn't know, but judging by the look on her face, my guess was coffin. It seemed to me she thought I had betrayed her somehow. Something had happened between us and she had taken offense. Like I said before, I don't understand women; don't know a man who does.

I had younger sisters, and my thought had always been they were needful things. I couldn't answer why, but I figured a woman, any woman was trouble. The type of trouble changed with age. Terri Moore would be no different.

In the morning light I could see she was pretty, and the problem was, she knew all too well. She had the idea that every boy or man she met would want her, and she was probably right. I adjusted my thinking, realizing such a girl would be a nightmare from the git-go. She'd be winking at some other boy when you weren't looking. Or starting a fight behind the back of any man she was with. I resigned myself to the idea right then and there it would not be me.

The thing I had not considered was how the war might change the habits of people. In bygone days, Scatter Creek had been a clearing house for local information, a rendezvous point. A lot could be learned from visiting here, but suddenly, the war seemed to change all that. No one was coming or going. I fretted a bit and tried to wrap my mind around the idea that things may have changed in my absence.

For two days I danced around the camp doing my best to stay shy of that girl. She wanted to go and I wanted to stay. At times I would walk away into the woods and return to find her and Michael sleeping or talking. As long as they didn't run off, I was happy. If they decided to take flight on their own, I would feel besmirched, but then I guess that's how Terri felt.

Chapter 4

In a pinch, a young man's imagination can do wonders. Here I was trying to get my name cleared of any wrong doing and it seemed I was having little luck. No one had stopped in that first day and the second nearly gone when an idea flashed in my brain.

"Terri, in the morning we'll ride for Gainesville. From there we'll go on to Peach Orchard. I can't sit here and wait for someone to show up. I've got to take my story to them."

"Well, it's about time. I need to be getting to my aunt's house."

"You'll be there by tomorrow afternoon," I promised. "In fact your aunt is the first person I'd like to tell, next to the sheriff."

"She should be, she's the founder of the Church of Christ in Gainesville, along with Uncle Clifton. He found good water at Peach Orchard and Aunt Sophie told him that was as far as she was going. Uncle Cliff has been felling trees and clearing swamp land ever since. He's brought in a small sawmill and ships a good bit of timber. If she doesn't have any clout in this area we're all in trouble. She's also the oldest living member of the Gainesville Church."

"What's their last name?"

"Cliff and Sophie Wagoner."

"I know them. My father use to buy lumber from him and even helped your uncle cut down a few of the big trees around our place."

The afternoon shadows leached the light from the forest. I noted the fact, but didn't say anything. The night before proved both were afraid of the dark, and to make matters worse, they were scared of anything moving in the middle of the night.

I didn't want to endure another night with these two 'fraidy cats, but it was too late for us to move out now. I settled down on my blanket roll and laid my head back. I knew the Starr's were nearly home and I dearly wanted to beat them to the punch when it came to sharing information with the local folks. There was little else I could do to proclaim our innocence. Mike had a bill of sale for his horse, but whether anyone would believe a piece of paper after the Starr's told their tale would be a miracle.

I went to sleep before the others could draw me into their paranoia about the darkness. I knew there wasn't anything in the dark what didn't exist in the daytime, but you couldn't tell these two anything when it came to night and day. They had their minds made up that a lion or some beast they couldn't see was going to have them for an evening snack.

When I awoke the next morning I was surrounded by chickens! I don't mean the feathered bird, I mean by two children who ought to know better than to be afraid of the dark. Terri had curled up against me on one side while Mike lay on the other. I took my booted foot and shoved Mike as hard as I could. I turned my head back the other way and looked directly into Terri's eyes.

"If you shove me like that, there'll be hell to pay," she said, her hand up, ready to slap me. My face was so close to hers I kissed her instead, and got slapped anyway.

"If you want to go to your aunt's house you'd better saddle up," I said.

On my feet after rubbing my stinging cheek, I picked up my saddle blanket and laid it on Jericho's back. Without turning my eyes her direction I went back for my saddle, then placed it on my horse blanket. I flipped the stirrup over the saddle, reached under his belly and pulled the girth strap through. I cinched it tight and went back for my blanket.

I noted the other two were quickly trying to catch up, but Terri was having trouble getting her saddle on the tall mule.

I finished rolling my blanket as I watched her get more and more frustrated. "If you'll give me a minute, I'll give you a hand."

"I don't want your help," she snapped back.

"Suit yourself, but you ain't never going to get that saddle on that mule."

"You watch me." She swung her saddle as hard as she could. The mule stepped out of the way and the saddle hit the ground with a thud. "Hold still you mangy ol' mule." She picked up the saddle and swung it again with everything she had. Again the mule sidestepped the attempt and looked back at her as if to say, "Over my dead body."

Terri was huffing and puffing by then, the saddle made heavier by her inexperience.

Tying my saddle bags and blanket roll to the back of my saddle, I watched a second or two before walking over, easily placing the saddle on the mule's back.

"Thank you."

"Don't thank me. The only reason I helped was because I couldn't stand to see your mule suffer."

Turning, I headed for Jericho. Right about then, I believe she hated me because I wasn't trying to court her, but I had stolen a kiss. From what I had seen she was a little too opinionated for me. I wanted a girl who would stand beside her man with a quiet strength, yet understand when I said something I meant it. Terri seemed a bit on the flagrant side for me. She was going to need some special attention I wasn't ready to give. Like a horse with a bad experience when broke to ride, it might take years to correct and I didn't have that much patience.

When I realized she didn't know what to do with the saddle once it was in place, I walked back over and finished securing it to the mule's back. I checked her reins and adjusted the too-long stirrups. Obviously, she hadn't been around horses much. Someone else must have saddled the mule when she left home.

While all of this fussing over her saddle was going on, Mike had crawled into his saddle and relaxed, watching the commotion from a safe distance. He knew we were fighting and he was smart to stay shy of it. I cupped my hands and lifted her into the saddle. She almost fell off the other side, but she regained her composure just in time to grab the saddle horn and pull herself back into position.

I stepped into my own saddle and we lit a shuck for Gainesville. I wanted to get this girl to her aunt's house,

but I had to stop by the county seat first. Little Miss Terri seemed unruly, cantankerous and disrespectful.

She rode the mule much better with her feet in the stirrups and didn't complain. If she had, I think I would have left her in the woods to find her own way. As things turned out, she finally shut up and rode. While Mike brought up the rear Terri stayed on my tail as we navigated the Scatter Creek trail into Gainesville.

An hour later we rode down Main Street. On the left was the Frank Scott store, Dr. Gregory's office, the Morrill Bakery. The Early Store was the next building then another doctor's office shared by Hopkins and Graham.

We'd come down the road from Scatter Creek, but the creek ran right through the middle of town. There were five small bridges in the community and if you stood at the right spot you could see every one of them at the same time.

Another doctor's office was across the street from the other two. The county seat had a raw population of around fifty people. Most folks in Greene County lived in the outlying areas like Terri's aunt. Miles from anywhere.

We found Sheriff Maurice Wright at the jailhouse. He was sipping on a cup of coffee when we invaded his office on the first floor.

"Sheriff, we need to talk with you."

"You children run along now. I have work to do."

He wasn't as busy as he wanted to be so I stepped forward. "Sheriff, I don't know if you remember me, but my name is Duke John Robinson."

He looked up from the paper he was reading then and locked eyes with me. "Duke John Robinson from over De'Laplaine way?"

"Yes sir, we want to report a hanging."

"I just bet you do. Captain Starr was in here yesterday afternoon and he said you are a horse thief, along with that other boy."

"They hung my pa and my grandpa," Mike said.

"That's what we do with horse thieves, young man."

"But they sold us those horses, I've got a bill of sale."

"You have a bill of sale which proves ownership?"

"Yes sir."

"Let me see it."

Mike fumbled for the document, but eventually pulled it out of his pocket and handed it over.

"That's Starr's signature," Sheriff Wright observed. "I'm going to have to look into the matter more closely son. I was told you stole the horses. This bill of sale trumps that. Where can I get in touch with you?"

Terri spoke up. "He'll be out at Peach Orchard for a while."

Folding the document, Sheriff Wright handed it back to Michael, a move I didn't expect. "All right, if I need you I'll come to Peach Orchard. Now, let me give you children some advice. Captain Starr is a known man in these parts. Proving murder won't be easy. I might not be able to press charges, but you stay clear from now on. I don't want youngsters interfering with what I have to do. You'll get your chance to talk when you come to court. And son, you'll need to bring that document to court. I'll notify you when, but before that there has to be a hearing. Do you understand?"

"Yes sir."

"I'll do what I can, but if you lose that document it's all over."

"I understand, sir."

"Get on out to Peach Orchard and I'll be in touch."

It took an hour and thirty minutes to hit the flats west of Crowley's Ridge. If a man didn't know the usual route through, he could end up staring at a dead end then have to backtrack. I knew my way around, and I think this ate at Terri more than anything. She didn't want to be beholden to me for anything, not even getting her through to her aunt's house.

The horseflies in the swamp got as big as hummingbirds and their bites drew blood every time they took a nip at the horses. Terri made the mistake of taking a swipe at one of them which had landed on the mule's neck. Already bothered by the constant biting, the slap spooked him and he took off like he'd been launched from a cannon.

Terri's hands were flailing in the wind looking for anything to hang onto when the mule raced up to a large pool of open water. He leaped into the air and when he landed Terri hit the water six feet away, her feet straight up in the air. The mule came down on the other side and never missed a beat. He was just plain gone.

By the time Michael and I got to her, she sat in the water sulking. I smiled down at her trying my best not to laugh out loud. I looked over at Mike and he was in the same state as me, stifling full blown laughter.

"Are you two going to sit there like a lump on a log or are you going to help me up?"

"I'm going after that mule," I said. I spurred my horse into the water where he'd splash her even more. On the other side, I never looked back. I knew she was cursing me, but I just didn't care.

I could hear her loud shrill voice echoing through the swamp after me, "Duke John Robinson you get back here!" She wasn't about to ride with me, so I had to get that mule.

He had left a pretty good trail and I had no trouble following him. He was standing in a small meadow cropping grass when I came up out of the swamp. I reached down, took his reins and he looked at me as if to say, "You're not taking me back to that woman, are you?"

Right then I thought maybe he understood me so I told him, "Come on, ol' boy. You aren't done yet, not by a long shot."

He pulled his head back the other way a couple of times to test the lead rope I had tied around the pommel of my saddle, then settled in behind me once he figured out he wasn't going anywhere but with me.

It took ten minutes to get back and when we did I was greeted by a much calmer young lady.

"I suppose I should thank you," she said.

"No, ma'am. I'm just sorry for the mule." I turned Jericho and rode out of the swamp, back onto the trail. I didn't much care if she got aboard the mule or walked. When I glanced back I saw Michael helping her up on the animal. I kept riding. That mule was not happy. I didn't figure she was going to stay in the saddle much longer, but I was wrong. Apparently, the two of them had come to an understanding for the time being. It wasn't long before we had the buildings of Peach Orchard in our sight.

It was at least fifteen miles the way we had to come through and around the swamp, but only ten or so if you were an eagle. There was a pair of eagle's which had a habit of living in the area, but I hadn't seen them today.

We had passed close enough to see the charred embers of what was once my home, but we didn't turn in that direction.

As soon as I dropped off little miss goody two shoes I was going to dig up my money and head west. I didn't much care what the Starr family did. I just wanted to head for the hills. The Rocky Mountains sounded awful good right then.

Now Peach Orchard wasn't much, just a few homes stacked together against the wind, but one of those homes belonged to Aunt Sophie and her Uncle Clifton. Between the three families which were there, they had managed to clear nearly fifty acres of swamp land for farming. They had in a good crop of corn and another of tobacco.

Aunt Sophie thanked us for getting Terri to her safely and then fed us like kings. I have to tell you, I hadn't eat like that in a long time. When I set up to the table, I took some of everything she placed in front of me, which consisted of fried okra, tomatoes, corn, bread, beef, and potatoes and gravy. Once I was a full, I almost fell asleep in my chair at the table while Terri told her aunt everything that was transpiring to the east.

"Them Yankees have crossed the river and have a camp near the farm," she said.

"Why didn't your mother come with you?"

"She said if she left the Yankee's would take everything."

"The Yankee's will take everything anyway," Aunt Sophie hissed. "What about your brothers and sisters?"

"They all went different directions. Ma insisted that we ride separate ways."

"That silly woman, she's scattered her children into the four winds."

That was all I remembered before I was dead to the world. Aunt Sophie woke me long enough to put me to bed. I was so tired I didn't even think of my horse.

She put a good breakfast in me the following morning, but I was ashamed of having passed out like I'd done. Humbled, I apologized for my rudeness.

Aunt Sophie said, "Don't let it bother you. I take it as a compliment you were able to sleep so easily under a strange roof."

"I haven't been under a roof in so long I just naturally forgot how comfortable the arrangement was."

"You burned your own house down," she said with a sudden realization. "I remember you now. Why did you do such a thing?"

"I didn't want anyone else to move in."

"The only person you seem to have deprived is yourself," Terri said.

"That may be. I know for certain no one else will ever live in the old house."

"What difference does it make? That's what I don't understand. People don't just burn down a house so no one else can live in it unless they have a good reason," Aunt Sophie argued.

"I had one. Let's just leave it at that."

Terri rolled her eyes. "You're one strange puppy, Duke Robinson."

"I might be, but I know what I'm doing and I know where I'm going."

"And where might that be," Aunt Sophie asked.

"I'm headed for the Rocky Mountains, but before I go I want to clear my name of any wrong doing."

"I'm listening," Aunt Sophie replied.

Yours truly, Terri and Michael were the only folks left in the house after the men lit out for work the next morning besides Aunt Sophie. As you can guess we were all sitting around the dining room table having our little discussion, and I thought things were hitting a little too close to home so I was glad for the sudden change in our conversation.

"The Starr's told Sheriff Wright that I stole one of their horses, but I didn't, I had only borrowed Sho-me long enough to get my saddle because Jericho had gone lame. Apparently, he wasn't hurt too bad because he followed me most of the way home. The Starr's found my saddle before I could get back to it and I had to run for my life because I had Ol' Sho-me leading him back to my saddle. I was knocked unconscious while trying to get away and when I came to Jericho was there to help me."

Michael nodded his head as I spoke. "He's telling the truth ma'am. My pa had won that horse in a poker game fair and square, but that Starr bunch hung my grandpa and my father a few days ago for horse thieves. It was cold-blooded murder."

"The Starr's have a lot of clout in these parts, but it's been dwindling since the start of the war. Sheriff Wright will want to know about this. Where's that bunch now?" Aunt Sophie asked.

"I set them afoot four days ago," I told her. "It seemed to me they needed to do some walking. They're home now."

"What did you do with their horses?"

"Michael and I turned them out to pasture on the Starr ranch."

"Young man, why are you still riding Sho-me?" she asked Michael.

"He may have been won in a poker game ma'am, but I have the bill of sale in my pocket."

"I see. Well, it appears as if Mr. Starr has some explaining to do. I'll send Cliff after Sherriff Wright when he gets in from the fields later today. In the meantime, you boys stay close to the house. If you're out wondering around the countryside, there's little we can do to protect you."

"None of that's necessary. We already spoke with Sheriff Wright. He's looking into the matter," I told her.

"Young man, it might do you good to know that Maurice Wright and Captain Starr are old friends. If you said anything to Sheriff Wright, it was probably dismissed the moment you told him."

"You mean he won't look into the matter?"

"He'll look into the matter, but I'm not sure what he'll do with information which might besmirch the Starr family reputation."

While this was going on I saw a smile appear on Terri's face and I knew she was having her way. She had two boys in the woodpile which she thought were pining for her love, but she couldn't have been more wrong. There was only one and it wasn't me. I learned later that Mike wasn't bellyaching for love either.

Two hours later, Cliff rode in from the fields for an early lunch. When he heard our account he mounted a different horse and headed for town.

Cliff would be gone until late the next day, maybe longer if Sheriff Wright wasn't in. The only way to get to town was a narrow road through the De'Laplaine Swamp. I was wishful to see my home place, even anxious, but Sophie Wagoner wasn't having any of it.

"You need to stay right here until we get this thing resolved," she said. "Besides, you can't go riding off anywhere until you've cleared your name."

I was setting on the front porch when she told me that. I knew she was right. Mike and Terri were out walking near the back of the house. He was picking wildflowers and handing them to her the last I saw of them. Suddenly a scream went up that would curl your hair. Before I could figure just what was happening, Terri came running around the corner of the house screaming.

"Aunt Sophie they're going to kill him!"

I didn't wait to hear her explanation I took off around the corner of the house and spotted the Starr bunch. They were beating the daylights out of Michael. I shucked my pistol and shot into the air.

"The next one of you that hit's him is going to be the first one to hell. Now back away before I change my mind and shoot you anyway."

They backed up and the two that had been holding the boy let him fall.

"You just had to do it didn't you?" I said. "You killed him."

"He ain't dead," old man Starr protested.

"No? Well he ain't here for the proceedings either. Pick him up and bring him up to the house."

They were all there, Captain Franklyn Starr, Bubba, Jupiter and Asa. What puzzled me was why they were

here in the first place? Had the sheriff told them where to find us?

I got behind them to make sure they didn't try anything funny. They lay Mike on the front porch and Mrs. Wagoner had a few words for them.

"If this boy dies, I'm going to see to it you all hang for murder. Captain, you've been the bull around here long enough. If you don't reign yourself in you're going to find the lot of you swinging from a rope. Like I said, you better pray this boy lives." She waved her shotgun in their direction. "Now get on home."

They started walking back around the house to their horses. Aunt Sophie and I followed with drawn weapons. They stepped into leather like the sorry bunch they were and headed down through the swamp.

To my estimation, we should have run into one another in Gainesville. Talk about a surprise. We'd not been in their plans at all. Now they had some adjusting to do. They knew we meant business, and even the Starr family knew better than to buck heads with the Wagoner's, who were well thought of by just about everyone in Greene County.

Chapter 5

Cliff Wagoner returned home the following day. Mike was still unconscious. I saw a man get mad then. When Aunt Sophie finished telling him the story of what had happened, his face was red as a beet. His own sons were off fighting in a war nobody wanted and violence had come to his doorstep.

I could see Uncle Cliff doing his best to fight the anger down, but the thought of Michael maybe dying in his house had him ready to extract some of his own justice.

"Sheriff Wright is ill equipped to deal with that Starr bunch," he said over supper. "We're going to have to get up a posse if that boy dies."

"I want to be in it," I said from my end of the table.

"You're nothing more than a boy, so mind your manners."

"I'll grant you that. But, I believe Captain Starr killed my Pa and I want to ride with you."

"Well now, that's the first time I've heard your Pa was killed."

"His body was never found. If he was alive he would've come home."

"You're probably right about that. All right Duke, if we have to round up the Starr family for murder you can ride with us, but you'll do as I say, you hear. I don't want any young'un popping off unexpectedly and getting someone killed. Least of all me."

46

"Yes sir."

Cliff looked down the table. "Pass me some more of them mashed potatoes honey."

The red hue faded from Mr. Wagoner's face slowly. I guess the conversation helped some. I didn't know Mr. Wagoner like I should know a neighbor that lived so close, but I liked him. In those days there weren't a lot of people in northeast Arkansas, and Dad had been a recluse of sorts. He didn't like other folks, he merely tolerated them. In a way, though, Clifton Wagoner was the same type of man as my father.

Our house had stood only five miles from here. Our closest neighbor would have been the Wagoner's. The two other homes in Peach Orchard belonged to Mr. Wagoner's brothers. Brett and his wife Dolly lived in one and Ervin and Pollyanna occupied the other. Tucker and Esmeralda or Ma and Pa as the brother's parents were known, lived with Brett and Dolly. They were of an age where they didn't do much but sit on the front porch in a rocking chair and while the day away.

Watching his family interact made me miss my own siblings. I hadn't seen them in a good while and wasn't even sure where to find them at this point. The way I figured, Pa had better be dead or he was going to have some awful powerful explaining to do when he showed up at home.

After supper I strolled around the yard. I had to make a stand in order to clear my name with the local authorities. That might be a challenge considering the proclivities of Sheriff Wright. I wanted to leave, but I knew the right thing for me to do was to have a little patience, do nothing wrong and wait the situation out. An

impatient spirit had destroyed more than one man's dreams and I didn't want any part of what might happen otherwise.

I watched the sun go down. While I'd been walking and thinking, the other folks had made themselves comfortable on the porch. When the shadows grew long, we went inside. Mosquitos were a special nuisance in this part of the country after sundown. The swamp was full of them and they were doing their best to carry me away.

When I awoke the next morning there was some improvement in Mike's condition. I knew the others were as relieved as I was. None of us had really taken a deep breath through the night, I was sure. When Mike opened his eyes, we were eating breakfast.

He looked up from his resting place in the front room and said, "What happened?"

Every head at the table turned to look his way. He was a pitiful sight with two black, almost swollen shut eyes, and a broken nose. He complained as he pushed himself up to rest on one elbow.

"You took a beating from that Starr bunch," Mr. Wagoner said.

Dismay clouded his face. "They took the Bill of Sale for Sho-me," he muttered.

"Won't do them no good anyhow. You've already relayed your story to the sheriff. He's heard what happened and they can't lay horse thief on you. In fact, they may be in more trouble than you right about now."

"But without a Bill of Sale I might as well be riding a stolen horse."

"I think we can clear matters up with the sheriff at Gainesville. His job is to deal with stuff like this and in your case, you have plenty of witnesses."

"But without the Bill of Sale, they'll get off scott-free!"

"Son, they aren't getting away with anything. Sheriff Wright knows all about your family. He'll get to the bottom of things," Mr. Wagoner promised.

Michael lay back lifeless as a rag doll. He might be better, but he had a long way to go to be okay again. I couldn't help but wonder if the sheriff tipped the Starr family to be sure and get that Bill of Sale back? Captain Starr had been pretty good friends with Sheriff Maurice Wright the last I knew. Suddenly I was not so trusting where Sheriff Wright was concerned.

I saddled up Jericho and told Aunt Sophie I was going to ride over and look at the old homestead. I mentioned I wanted to be alone and when I left out that's exactly what I was. I had some thinking to do, but I also had to see about recovering some of Pa's money. It was a relief that I had my belongings back in my possession. Whether by luck or by chance I wasn't sure and didn't care. I had them and that's all that mattered.

It was a foggy, damp morning. A slight haze hung at treetop level, the ground air on the cool side. I navigated the old road and soon I came to the old trail leading to the homestead. It was a good feeling to be home and I settled into daydreaming about when Ma and Pa were both there as I made my way through the last bunch of trees before reaching the yard.

Suddenly I heard voices up ahead and I brought up short. Someone was on the old place. It didn't sound like one or two people, but a bunch of folks. I eased forward

until I could see them plain. Johnny Rebs. I eased forward. I wanted what was mine and not even soldiers were going to stop me.

I made my presence known by riding on into the camp. They pulled up short and watched me as I stepped down off Jericho and tied him to a nearby tree. When I turned around I was addressed by their captain.

"Who are you?"

"Name's Duke John Robinson. You're on my land."

"You don't look old enough to be a land owner," the captain said.

"When your father dies, what is his becomes yours does it not?"

"It does."

"Then you're standing on my land, and welcome."

"Have you eaten?"

"Yes sir, I ate already."

"We're just making temporary camp. My name is Captain Nathanial Bowlin. Folks hereabouts call me the Swamp Fox."

"I've heard of you, and you're still welcome."

In two short years Nathanial Bowlin had become a legend in these parts. He was called the Swamp Fox and he had earned the name fittingly.

"Set up to the fire. We have coffee on."

"Thank you, don't mind if I do."

"You haven't seen any Yankee's hereabouts have you?"

"No sir, not since I left Missouri last week."

"You saw Yankee's in Missouri?"

"Yes sir, they were camped near Belle City. They tried to get me to join their outfit, but I'm no Yankee," I admitted.

"Good man. Them Yankee's are taking in way too much territory. I think me and the boys will mosey off up that way and see if we can't find an encounter. Last time we struck them they were closer to Poplar Bluff."

"They had with them a pretty good commander by the name of William Tecumseh Sherman," I said.

"General Sherman, ha!" He turned to his men and yelled. "Finish your meal men, we ride for Missouri and the chance to engage a high ranking commander."

There were about thirty men in this unit, but I'd heard tell Nathanial Bowlin often had two or three hundred riding with him. Everyone in the Greene County area knew about the growing legend of the Swamp Fox. He would ride up into Missouri, strike a Yankee encampment and leave the area before they could muster a response. Many times the Yankee's would try to follow Bowlin and his men into the swamps of Arkansas only to be swatted down like flies. In short order the Yankee's would turn and run every time the losses became too great. At least that was the way the story was told me.

I shared a good hot cup of coffee with the commander and then he and his men pulled up stakes, headed for Missouri as if their tails were on fire. As I watched them go I knew they were the type of men who would not fail in their mission whatever it was.

As the dust settled I began to look around the place calculating just how I could dig up all that money. It occurred to me that if the men who had just left knew they had been sitting on thousands of dollars in buried

treasure, they wouldn't have lit out so quickly. As things stood, what they didn't know was good for me.

I went over to my horse and pulled out my rifle, thankful I was alone once again. The sky was clearing, but while the clouds appeared to be evaporating, they were only moving higher to regroup. I had seen them do such a thing before and I knew it would be raining cats and dogs by late afternoon.

That was Arkansas weather. There wasn't anything a person could do about it. All you could do was mind yourself and try not get caught in it. I looked into the distance and could still see my old tree house Pa had built for me deep in the swamp. The structure was a good half mile away, yet obviously still there.

That old tree house was a comfort. We had built it on my tenth birthday. While I wasn't the only sibling to use it, the house had been mine.

A short handle shovel was a tool most folks carried, so no one had said anything about the shovel on my saddle. Most every man carried one. When traveling out in the wild, a shovel was a handy thing when a man needed to use the bathroom. It was customary to dig a small hole, use the bathroom and then cover the evidence. They had no idea my shovel was for digging up money. Often a unit might only have two or three shovels among them, but the men who had just left each had one.

I paced off the first marked tree distance and started digging. Shortly I uncovered a mason jar. The money was still here. I paced off the second marked tree location and dug up that jar. There was about a thousand dollars among the two, but there was more, much more.

I kept digging. Here and there they seemed a little light but for the most part they were full. By the time the showers started to move in I had near all of Pa's money placed in my saddle bags. I went back to get one last jar and when I kneeled down to dig my world exploded in a thousand bright colors, then slowly faded to black.

When I came to it was pouring rain. I had no idea how long I'd been out, but the instant before I passed out, I recognized Bubba Starr. Once again the Starr family was cutting a wide swath in business which was none of their affair. I was mad clean through and when I sat up I got madder. My horse was gone, my weapons were gone and I was abandoned, left for dead no doubt. Except for the anger bubbling hot in my belly, I was cold and lonely right then.

In the rain I could no longer see the treehouse, but I knew where it was. Picking up my hat up off the ground I headed in the direction of my old playgrround. My head swam, my ears rang and the rain pounded my head into unimaginable pain.

As I neared the treehouse I could tell someone was already there. Climbing the ladder my expectations lead me to believe Bubba Starr had also sought shelter here. Instead, my mouth fell open as I beheld my father. He was wet, bloody and shivering. While blood covered the floor of the treehouse, I could see his chest rise and fall. He was alive.

"Pa, what are you doing here?" I scrambled to him, and tried to see where the blood was coming from. He'd bleed to death if I didn't stop it somehow.

Struggling to talk, he managed to say, "I needed shelter, somebody burned the house. I'm sorry son."

"You've nothing to be sorry for Pa. What happened to you?"

"I was coming home. Captain Starr he shot me."

"Captain Starr did this to you?"

Pa choked and coughed, but shook his head yes. "Son, promise me you won't go after him."

"He's been figuring ways to hang me for the last week. Now Bubba's stolen our money. All of it. Don't tell me not to go after him, cause they're putting a burr under my saddle real fast. They've taken everything including Jericho."

Pa nodded and I could see in his eyes that he was in more pain from the loss of his savings than the bullet hole.

"Pa, you rest up. I'm going build a fire down below in order to get some heat up here."

"All right, son."

I climbed down the ladder and gathered the driest wood I could find. Thank God the tree house was about ten by ten and low to the ground, otherwise there would be no fire to build. As things stood I had good cover and a stash of dry firewood under the house. I had learned early on that if'n I wasn't real careful I could burn down the entire struture.

It took me thirty minutes in the steady downpour, but I eventually got the fire going and went up to check on Pa, He was sound asleep, but he was still breathing.

I lay down beside him in order to gauge the warmth coming through the floor and to get myself warm. My head still pounded and my ears rang. I eventually fell asleep next to my father in the tree house we had built before being separated three years before.

I had some crazy dreams that evening. Someone was always drawing a gun on me, but somehow I talked them into putting it away or I shot them before they could pull their own trigger. Always I came away clean, not a scratch on me. It was the strangest of dreams, but I didn't mind the idea that I was always the winner. One of the men who had drawn on me in the middle of the night was Sheriff Wright himself, and I palmed my gun then buried him. I knew it was child's play, that in a real gunfight I was likely to lose, but it was a comfort to at least know that in my dreams I was invincible.

Chapter 6

I studied my Pa in the early morning hours from the confines of our tree house. Where had Pa been? What was so important that he hadn't contacted us? I could think of nothing which would explain his absence these last three years. I tried every scenario a boy could think of as I watched my father labor and struggle for each breath, but in the end I could divine no answer. Where had he been, what had he done to end up shot by the likes of Captain Franklyn Starr?

There was no question I would have to go get some help. The closest help would be at Peach Orchard. The Wagoner's would probably be looking for me by now. The rain had subsided, the sun was coming out and it was a new day. I tried to wake Pa, but he was unconscious so I shimmied down the ladder, stirred the fire to kindle a new blaze, added a small log to keep the heat rising and started for the Wagoner's.

My horse being gone there was nothing to do but run. I had to run all the way or Pa might die. I took off down the muddy trail from De'Laplaine to Peach Orchard, but soon realized how difficult such a task might be. Running on dry ground is one thing, running in a mud filled swamp is quite another. Ten minutes into my attempt I realized what it felt like to die. My chest was heaving in great gasps, my legs felt like iron beneath me after just a few minutes. The mud hanging onto my boots caused a struggle I could never have imagined. Several times my

feet came out from under me landing me face down in the mud or on my rear. With more mud caked on me, the difficulty of my task grew. As I neared the halfway point I knew this to be the hardest thing I had ever the joy of doing for there was no joy in it. My father's life hung in the balance.

Just before noon I struggled into the yard to find Aunt Sophie sitting on the front porch peeling potatoes. "Looks like somebody lost their horse."

"I beg your pardon, ma'am," I managed between huffs of breath, "but the only reason I lose anything of late seems to be because of the Starr family. Bubba hit me over the head and took everything, but I found Pa. He's been shot. He needs a doctor."

I had her attention now. She dropped that bowl of potatoes and jumped up, barking orders this way and that. In five minutes her husband was riding for one of the doctors at Gainesville.

There were several doctors in Gainesville. Back then it was customary for the doctors to ride in a particular circuit, sort of like a preacher man. They each had their own clients, but between them they serviced the entire Greene County area. I didn't care which one they brought back so long as they brought one of them.

I settled down to eat and told my story in more detail. I explained about meeting Nathanial Bowlin, getting robbed after digging up all of our money and finding Pa. Aunt Sophie asked a question from time to time, but never did she push matters. She just wanted some details.

By nightfall my father was in the house at Peach Orchard, but he was still unconscious, fighting for his very life. It seemed to me Pa had lost way too much blood

before the doctor arrived. Dr. Webb had done all he could and would stay through the night. If all went well, he said Pa would be awake sometime in the next day or two.

That's how we all went to sleep that evening, in hopes that Pa would get better by morning now that the bullet was out of him and he was sewn up tight. I struggled with my dreams that night. I struggled and tossed, turning in my sleep. There was nowhere for me to hide.

When I awoke the next morning I went in to see my father. He was breathing hoarsely, struggling for each breath, but he was still wasn't conscious. About noon as I held onto his hand he came to. He pulled on my hand and then looked me in the eye.

"We sure played hob, boy."

"Pa, what's going on? Why does Captain Starr want to kill us?"

"It's an old feud son. I should have told you about it long ago, but I didn't want you or your brothers and sisters involved. It seems you're in it now, whether you want to be or not." Again he squeezed my hand.

"But Pa, where have you been?"

"I've been aboard ship, sailing the seven seas these last three years, but not by choice. I was shanghaied. Captain Starr saw to it I was sold into servitude aboard the Night-crawler down at New Orleans. I should still be there had not I escaped while in port last month."

"You mean Captain Starr did all this to you?"

"Yes son, but I don't want you to go fighting him, for there is not one ounce of decency in him. He wouldn't hesitate to do the same to you."

"Or hang me," I said.

"That bad is it?"

"Yes Pa, things are that bad."

"Well, I guess he burned the house too, it was ashes when I got home, looked like it had been for a while."

"Pa, they have our money. I dug it up two days ago and Bubba hit me over the head and took it all."

He coughed then and mostly he coughed up blood. Doc Webb was there immediately to take charge of the situation. "You need to rest, Mr. Robinson. I know you want to talk, but you need to rest."

"All right doc, have it your way," and he coughed again.

We retreated to the other room and settled down at the table. The rest of the folks in the Wagoner household seemed to be busy about their chores, so Doc Webb decided to talk with me.

"Son, if I were you I would stay beside your father as much as possible. He's in worse shape than I thought. If he takes on any type of fever we might lose him."

"Isn't there anything I can do?"

"Just what I am telling you. Stay by his side and don't let him think he's alone. Sometimes, having a family member by your side makes all the difference in the world. So you stand by him."

"Yes sir, but the Starr bunch sure needs a reckoning."

"They'll get it, son, but right now you need to be here for your father."

"And I will be. I don't have anything else to do but see him well."

"I'm not going anywhere either. Maybe together we can see him through," Doc said.

Suddenly I found myself listening intently to Doc Webb while he spun yarns of old, telling me of ancient

myths, unusual remedies and things of interest. His countenance was that of an old troubadour, the village story teller. I listened with undivided attention as he talked about the Roman Empire, the Celtic's and Alexander the Great.

"When the Pilgrim's landed at Plymouth Rock, they found forts all up and down the eastern seaboard, though burned to the ground by local Indian's, they uncovered Roman coins at every site so when they say Alexander the Great conquered the world, I believe he truly conquered the entire known world, and two thousand years ago, this part of the world was known, but something happened and people lost touch with it."

"Well, it's a cinch they didn't have the Pony Express back then, and they didn't have the telegraph wire," I observed.

"Duke, you sure have a unique way of putting things."

"What do you mean?"

"I mean, I have been derelict in my duties. I should have already sent a message to the Sheriff at Gainesville. He needs to know about such things."

"I believe he already knows," I answered.

"How can that be," the doctor asked.

"He's in on it. He and Franklyn Starr are good friends."

"You are saying Sheriff Wright is corrupt."

"I am not sure, but things are pointing that direction."

Suddenly Pa coughed and choked in the other room and we jumped up to aid him. I knew when I saw all the blood Pa was in trouble. Doc Webb knew it too. Pa was still bleeding inside.

"Son, go get me a pan of water."

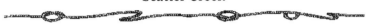

I didn't ask what for; I just did what I was told. My Pa was in trouble and I didn't want him to die. I was only a few minutes getting the water Doc Webb asked me for, and Pa had been coughing up blood the whole time.

"You hold his hand Duke, and don't let go."

I grabbed Pa's hand in both of mine. Doc Webb worked on him then, opening him up again and rooting around in Pa's body like he was searching for something, and he found it too. It was another bullet.

"I only saw one hole. Somehow both bullets went in the same place but took different paths. This one was lodged close to his heart. If you know how to pray you had better do it, son. He's in trouble like no man I ever saw, and still breathing."

I knew Pa had an ironclad constitution, but the question remained—was such a constitution enough to see a man through? His hand felt cold and clammy to the touch. His breathing was raspy and jerky. At times he seemed to stop breathing altogether, then when I thought he had passed away, he would resume breathing again.

With words intended to guide me, fear became my new status. Fear my father was about to die while I looked on, knowing there was nothing I could do. While Doc was cleaning out the bloody pan I held onto my father's hand. He fought to extract a single breath from the air in the room, then fight to take another one. While he struggled to breathe, I prayed for my father's deliverance from the grim reaper which seemed to besiege the atmosphere in the room.

If my father lived, I didn't see any way I could tell him I was the one who burned down our home. Such a thing would likely kill him on its own or make him hate me.

How could I tell him? I had no excuse. Now that Pa was home, no explanation I could create seemed adequate. I was at a loss to explain any of my actions to my father. Our family was scattered to the four winds and I didn't have the first clue where my brothers and sisters were living. In fact I hadn't made an effort to keep our family together at all, what now seemed a major failure on my part.

What would Pa think when he came around? How would he feel when he learned I had not been able to sustain the family, lost all of our money and burned down the house we once called home? I was feeling about as tall as a two day old tadpole.

I felt guilty as if I'd betrayed the entire family while sitting beside Pa's bed holding onto his hand. I could hardly breathe myself for choking on my past actions, struggling for every breath I could pull from the stifling atmosphere.

"Where are your brothers and sisters," Pa managed to whisper.

I looked at him and my thought was, he wasn't going to make it.

"I don't know, Pa."

"Promise me you will find them."

"I'll find them Pa, if it's the last thing I do."

He coughed some more then, losing his breath for a moment, then gained it back.

"Franklyn Starr burned down our home, I'm certain of it," he managed between breaths. "That no account shanghaied me, sold me aboard ship as a common slave."

"Pa, you need to rest,"

"I will son, like never before."

I had no way of knowing what he meant, but suddenly he was quiet. About two minutes later I realized his hand was getting colder. I jerked back my own hand and yelled for Doc Webb, falling over backward in my chair as I did so. Pa was gone. I never knew how quickly a person's body assumed room temperature upon death, but how quickly I learned. Death was something I had never witnessed firsthand, yet suddenly that had changed.

My first real thought was—I wouldn't have to explain my actions to Pa. The most selfish thought I could have at such a time. Relief set in, yet more prevalent, my shame as well, ready to berate me for my thoughts. I was ashamed of my unexpected actions and feelings, such degradation I could never tell a soul.

Doc Webb came into the room and looked down at my father. "I'm sorry, son. I did all I knew how. Had I realized he had two bullets in him he might be alive right now."

"I don't blame you, Doc. It's them Starr's. They're to blame for my father's death and I'm going to see to it they pay."

"Now hold on son, revenge never did a lick of good for anyone. You need to know revenge is the lowest form of human behavior on this planet."

"Maybe, but I'm going to get me some."

"You might want to make certain and bury your father first."

"I'm not going to wait around here for Bubba to blow all Pa's money. I'm going after Bubba soon as Pa is in the ground."

"You're going to get yourself killed."

"No, sir. I'm going to settle an old score with the Starr family once and for all or my name isn't Duke John Robinson."

The house filled with people then. Mrs. Wagoner started cooking and the men took Pa outside to the front porch, wrapped him in a blanket, then went to work to build a coffin. There was no graveyard in Peach Orchard at the time, so Pa was going to be the first body planted there. I walked around sulking a good deal, not wanting to talk to anyone.

Finally I sat down on the front porch and the dog which belonged to the Wagoner family came up to me and rested his head in my lap. His name was Rebel. He had a small rebel flag around his neck for a collar and everyone knew who's dog he was. As I sat there a plan began to develop in my mind. As devious a plan as man or boy ever envisioned, but I was want-full toward revenge and I wanted to savor the sweet taste.

If memory served me correctly, Bubba Starr had an old wolf-hound, a grey looking dog which was half German Shepard and half wolf named Joker. The plan I had in my head involved making the dog mine. Now I know the Starr family didn't feed the dog, for they wanted him to be independent and not count on being fed, so if my guess was right, all I needed to do was feed him proper and he'd follow me anywhere I wanted to go. Three years is a long time and the dog could be dead for all I knew.

I also wanted my horse, saddle, weapons, and my money back, but the dog would be first. I needed that dog, provided it still lived. Rebel was not mine and never would be, but Joker, I was going to make him mine. He

was named because the first thing he ever treed was a lynx. The second time he treed, he cornered a panther, and suddenly he learned when was a good time to run, because that second animal was king of the local swamp and taught Joker how to outrun such a thing as a swamp panther. Nine times out of ten when Joker treed, it wasn't a coon at all, but a cat of some sort.

Now, I was saddened at my father's recent death, but I was also glad of the fact he wasn't suffering anymore. Whether or not I was the cause of the suffering didn't seem to matter. All things being equal, he was in a better place now. I knew I would miss him more now than I had for a while, because he had reappeared, even if only for a brief time. At least now I knew what had happened to him. And that he hadn't left us because he'd wanted to.

The thought in the back of my mind however was quite simple; there was fixing to be a showdown. The only thing which was unanswered seemed to be the location in which said showdown would take place. The Starr family had done me wrong one too many times, and now I could add Pa's death to the long list of trouble they had heaped upon me.

Usually when someone snaps it's a sudden thing, but with me, this inequity had been a slow boil for several years. The pot was hot now and the lid was fixing to blow. I knew deep down where I stood and if I was to have a future at all I had to stand up for what was right. I had to stand against the damage done to me and my family and I had to win. I didn't figure no way it was going to be easy.

Chapter 7

We buried Pa that evening and I saddled up after supper. I didn't make any show of hanging around. I borrowed Ol' Sho-me from Michael and told him I'd be back come morning. I had some investigating to do which required the cloak of darkness. I wanted to know a few things and I didn't want any help which might slow me down or trip me up.

First off, I put some food in those saddle bags, but not just for me, for the dog which belonged to Bubba Starr. My plan was to feed the old wolf-hound, but in my heart I knew the dog was not more than four, maybe five years old. The dog would be in his prime.

The Starr Family lived south and west from Peach Orchard. If a man was to go straight west from the orchard, he'd end up in Pocahontas. The Starr family didn't live that far west, but maybe half way and then south for a few miles. I couldn't imagine just how they got their land, but I was beginning to think they stole it, much like everything else they seemed to put their hands on.

Now, traveling in a swamp at night is a tricky thing unless you know your way around. I knew the area, but I hadn't been in the swamps around De'Laplaine for at least three years. De'Laplaine was one of the first names given by the French explorers who passed through these parts more than a hundred years before. Not wanting to make a mistake, I rode for the old homestead. From there I could

navigate my way through the swamp, though three years is a long time and things do change.

A couple of times during the evening I found myself about to make a wrong turn. Of course, I would recognize this fact almost immediately and correct my course. It was an old trail through the swamp, but fallen trees and large tree limbs had in places made following the trail difficult. They also had the effect of throwing me off my path.

Just before midnight I stepped down from Ol' Shome and tied him off on a fallen tree limb. I walked the last hundred yards to the edge of the tree line in order to survey the Starr Ranch. All was quiet, and the lights were out while I looked on. That wolf-hound was there, I could see him lying on the front porch.

As I watched from the edge of the swamp I realized there were two things I could do tonight. I could steal my horse back, and maybe even get my saddle and rigging. It looked like several saddles were resting on the fence post of the corral rather than in the tack room of the barn. If one of them was mine, I was going to saddle up Jericho and ride for home.

The first problem I had was the dog. Joker would start barking if I didn't do things just right. As I sat there under the large cypress tree I began to wonder how I could get Joker to come to me. If I called him I might be heard from the start. If I just started for the corral he would surely alert the entire house and the men in the bunkhouse.

Wouldn't those same men be standing guard? I cringed at the thought. If they were standing guard, I had no chance at all. Unexpectedly, Joker stood up and sniffed the air. My intuition said it was me; the guilt laden odor

on the evening breeze was one Duke John Robinson. The wind was blowing from east to west on this night and that was a very rare event in this northeast corner of Arkansas.

Only a complete dummy would assume the wolf-dog could not smell him. I watched as he gave the air a couple of more sniffs, then he began to howl. I held still waiting to see if anyone near the house responded. After a couple of deep howls he jumped down from the front porch and headed my way. I started back for Ol' Sho-me and dug into my saddle bags for food.

When I got back to the cypress tree, Joker had stopped about half way across the open field, sniffing the night air once more. I sat down under the tree and began to whisper so that only the dog could hear me. My hope was that he would remember my voice. It had been a long time, yet once a dog got used to a voice, they didn't seem to forget.

Every coonhound has its own distinct voice. One will be a low pitched groan while another might be a high pitched squall. No two are alike. When a coon dog treed, he or she would howl until you showed up to relieve them. A real good coon dog knew when you showed up to heel and wait on you. Joker was supposed to be that good only he didn't find many coons. He usually took in after a cat.

Coon was good eating, much like possum, catfish and cornpone. A good cook could make any local swamp varmint into tasty treats. There was a trick to it, but many of the lady's here in northeast Arkansas prided themselves on their cooking prowess. The Greene County Fair was held every year and there wasn't much for kids to do but taste different pies, chase a greased piglet or eat the food of the day which often times was possum, catfish

or cornpone. There were always sack races for the kids, shooting matches for the men and a cook-off for the women. This event was always held at Gainesville which was the Greene County seat.

I hummed and sang to myself in a stealthy voice while noticing Joker took a few steps in my direction, then stopped. He howled again, so I took this as an omen. I dropped the food I had on the ground then headed for Ol' Sho-me. Tonight was not going to see the success I had been hoping for, but I knew tomorrow night would come and when I stepped into the saddle on Ol' Sho-me I could see the dog had gotten to the tree where I had been sitting. He was watching me.

I rode away confident he would have a good meal and remember me tomorrow evening. It was my hope and prayer that my plan wouldn't take more than one or two more evenings to achieve results. The longer my plan took, the more risk I was apt to be taking.

I rode back into the yard at sunup and found Michael there to greet me. "Well, how did things go?"

"As well as a fellow could expect."

"What are you plans for today?"

"Sleep. I'm going to eat something and then I'm going to sleep."

"There's food on the table. I'll take care of Ol' Sho-me. You go eat while the getting's good."

I didn't argue because I was tired and hungry. I ate what Aunt Sophie had put on the table and then I ate a little more. She was proud of the way I was eating, yet I was somewhat shameful.

"It's good to see two growing boys eating well," she said while picking up the dishes. "Your cot is waiting for you in the other room."

There was no need to show me where the cot was, I knew the spot well. Kicking off my boots I lay down and went to sleep with my next breath.

At noon I awoke to eat lunch and then went outside to pet Rebel. I was still tired from my nighttime of prowling the previous evening.

After supper I saddled up Ol' Sho-me and headed for the Starr ranch once again. I took my time keeping a wary eye in all directions. As before, I rode to the old homestead first then began my trek from there. Two hours after dark I stopped in the same place as the night before, only tonight I had brought food with me to the tree. When I got to the old cypress, I saw Joker only about fifty yards away. He was quiet, yet observant. When he smelled the food he cautiously started toward me without a sound.

There were still lanterns glowing in the house, but as Joker neared cypress tree the lamps were put out. The one at the bunkhouse remained on for a while longer, yet Joker enjoyed the food I had brought to him with no thought for what was going on back at the house. When he finished he trotted away about twenty yards then sat down and looked back at me.

"It's all right boy, come here," I whispered, but my voice seemed to spook him and he trotted off a little further.

I was patient, waiting for what I wanted. I wanted Joker, and I wanted him to never look over his shoulder toward the home he now had. For this I was prepared to

do whatever was necessary. I went back to Ol' Sho-me and retrieved more food. As I sat down, Joker edged closer to me. I stuck my hand out and offered another morsel to him. He darted forward enough to empty my hand and then retreated with meat in jaw. In only a moment he swallowed the food and looked at me like he wanted more.

That was all I had for him on this evening, so I got up and started for Ol' Sho-me. I took up the reins and stepped into the saddle. Joker was there to watch me and when I turned in the direction of the old homestead, he took a few steps toward me then stopped. I kept looking over my shoulder to see if he would follow, but he did not. He was content having been fed, so he stood his ground and watched me ride away.

The following evening I stopped short of the cypress tree and waited in the woods. Sure enough Joker came wondering in about ten that evening. Rather than give him food right off I rode back toward the old homestead with him sniffing my trail. I surely had food for him in my saddle bags, but I wasn't about to give it to him without first getting him away from the house.

We hung onto the trail which led home and when I entered the clearing of the old homestead I stepped down to get the food. I fed him good right there, and then I moved, letting him rest easy below the old tree house. An hour before sunup I was in the saddle headed home.

The next evening I stopped at the old home place and laid out my bag of goodies. I put their aroma into the air and it wasn't long until Joker came wondering down the trail. He was looking for me now. I fed him again and went to sleep in the old tree house. I left an hour before

sunup and the dog appeared sad to see me go. I called him several times, but he wasn't yet ready to follow me.

On my fifth try he was waiting for me at the tree house. I was happy, but cautious too. That dog was beginning to make a regular trail through the swamp and if anyone found it I was going to be in for trouble.

I dismounted and gave him half of what I had, then I crawled up in my tree and went to sleep. Joker was still there when I woke up an hour before sunup, so I fed him while I set my saddle back on Ol' Sho-me. He knew me now, he knew I was the bearer of good tidings and when I started for home he was trotting right along beside me. I smiled to myself at the thought of having the best hound in northeast Arkansas, and I smiled some more when I realized that owners don't choose their dogs, the dogs choose their owners. Joker had chosen me over the Starr family and I was going to see to it that he stayed with me.

There weren't too many folks in this part of the country who weren't up for a good feud now and again, and I had just started one. What I had no way of knowing was that my feud with Bubba Starr was not the only feud under way in Greene County at that moment. Captain Nathanial Bowlin and Sheriff Wright had a feud of their own, building a full head of steam.

I was tired again, but with instructions to feed my dog along with Rebel I went to sleep on my cot. As I slept, visions of Bubba having a big party with Pa's money danced through my head. I woke up in a cold sweat. Bubba Starr was invading my life while I slept. I didn't know what to do about such a thing but tackle the problem head on. My horse, saddle and guns were still in his possession, not to mention the money. When I got up

it was late afternoon and Joker was lying on the front porch. I petted him and wrestled with the ideas in my head. I had to get my horse back.

"Michael, I need to borrow Sho-me one more time," I said as I headed for the barn.

"What for?"

"I'm going after my horse and saddle tonight. Joker won't give me away, he's mine now."

"I sure hope you know what you are doing."

I looked at him and said, "Me too!"

I stopped by Pa's grave for a minute and then I put Sho-me on the trail to the Starr Ranch. My wolf-hound was following right along, like he wasn't about to miss whatever action I had planned. I tossed him a hunk of dried venison every once in a while to ensure his loyalty and soon found myself at the Starr holdings.

The sun was setting and it appeared everyone was inside for supper. I'd heard the dinner bell a few minutes before and if my guess was right, every able body man on the ranch was eating. I had to wait though. I wasn't so good that I could steal back my horse in broad daylight. What I had to do required the devil's veil.

Faith in your ability or God is one thing, stupidity is quite another. If I tried to take Jericho in broad daylight, that would be stupidity. In fact, I could just see God sitting up there on his throne in heaven laughing so loud that he busted a gut while the entire Starr family surrounded me with loaded weapons. What I didn't understand was that God was laughing heartily at my expense already. As I sat beneath my cypress tree, I watched the front door of the house open up and my little sister Sarah stepped out onto the front porch. I did a

double take, but it was her. She was a little bigger now, but there was no mistaking the way she moved. My little sister was being raised by the Starr family!

I didn't budge until everyone had their back to me, then I scurried around behind that tree to get out of the line of sight. I was wishful to be away. Suddenly my horse didn't seem so all fired important anymore. They had my youngest sister. I made my way back to where Ol' Sho-me waited in the woods, and when I got there, Bubba was waiting for me.

"I knew something was going on. That dog was getting awful lazy. Now, I'm fixing to kill you with your own gun."

I looked down and saw the gun he was wearing. It was mine, just like he said. There's a time for talking and a time for shooting. I just didn't figure there was anything I could say at this point which would make a lick of difference, so I dragged iron and shot Bubba right where he stood, using a gun I had borrowed from Mr. Wagoner. I hadn't hit Bubba hard enough to kill him, but I sure bled him some. Then, without waiting, I unbuckled my gun belt from around his waist and bent a little farther to put the barrel of my pistol up his nose.

"What did you do with the money?"

I shoved the end of the muzzle up against his nose a little harder.

"I buried it," he said, panting.

"Where?"

"At Scatter Creek, but you'll never find it."

"You had better pray I do," I said and I stepped into my saddle. I left on the run because I could hear everyone

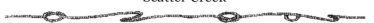
in the Starr household headed my way. I didn't figure on being present when they found Bubba.

I lit a shuck and you know what? Joker was right there with me. Bubba was yelling at the dog to stay, but the dog wouldn't listen to him anymore. He was mirroring every track my horse made through the De'Laplaine swamp. Well, I had my pistol back anyway.

When I got to our old homestead back in the swamp I kept right on riding, headed for Scatter Creek. I might not ever find my money, but if it was buried like Bubba said, I suspected the dog was witness to the event. There was no way I could prove it one way or another, but that was what I kept telling myself. I tossed Joker some meat and kept on riding. If I was lucky, that new dog of mine would lead me right to the spot.

I knew he wouldn't lead me straight to it for he had no idea what it was I really wanted, but if he got close to where the money was actually buried, he would likely sniff around the site for a bit and possibly tip me off as to the whereabouts. The following day as we made our way down the loneliest stretch of Scatter Creek, that's exactly what happened.

I saw him sniffing the ground in an area which didn't make a lick of sense, and rode up to see what he was paying attention to. It was a freshly dug and filled in hole. Stepping down from Ol' Sho-me I pulled out Michael's short shank shovel and began to dig. There, less than a foot down was my money. My dog had led me straight to it. I petted him and told him he was a good boy. Then I broke the jars open and stored the money in my saddle bags, giving the remaining food to Joker. He was as happy to get that food as I was to get my money back.

When we left Scatter Creek I skirted the county seat and headed north toward the Missouri line. This was about twenty-five miles out in the swamp once you were off Crowley's Ridge, headed straight north from where I was located. My intent was Peach Orchard, but not from the south, I was coming home from the north, not wanting to run into anyone who might intercept me.

Fact was the Wagoner family was probably getting worried about me by now, not to mention Michael, for I had been borrowing his horse for the last week, but it couldn't be helped. They had given me some leeway because my father had just passed, but such hospitality would dry up fast unless I proved myself. Getting my money back as well as my *adoption* of the dog would prove me for the time being.

When I reached the Knobel fork which was nothing more than a fork in the road located in the middle of a swamp, Captain Nathanial Bowlin was there with at least thirty men. He welcomed me into his camp along with my dog. They had venison on the fire, beans in a big pot and they had just hit the Yankees up in Missouri the day before.

"I sure do wish you'd join me, Duke. I could use a good scout like you," he said as we sipped our coffee by the fire.

"I would like to sir, but I have to find my family. Pa died a few days ago and I swore I would locate my brothers and sisters. I've got to keep my promise."

"A young man has got to do what is on his mind to do," he said. "Just the same, if you ever change your mind, you'd be learning from the best."

"I'll keep that in mind sir."

They rode away an hour later and I headed on to Peach Orchard with Joker trotting right alongside of me. I had been nervous with that money in my saddlebags, but I shouldn't have been. I was among friends whenever Nathanial Bowlin was around.

At the Knobel house we once again turned southwest toward Peach Orchard. I skirted the house at Knobel, not wanting to arouse anyone. While I could see the roof in the distance rising into the trees, I didn't want to speak with a soul. It wasn't long before we were clear of the house headed down to Aunt Sophie's place.

I started getting a funny look from my dog about that time, and I could almost hear what he was thinking. Why was it necessary to travel thirty-five to forty miles to go ten? Well, I didn't have any kind of explanation for him that would matter, but he quit looking at me funny when Aunt Sophie fed him that evening. Suddenly I was forgiven.

Joker curled up under the front porch as soon as he'd finished eating. He was out like a lamp. I wasn't far behind him, but Rebel was keeping his distance. He had decided that his place was across the way under Brett and Dolly's front porch. The fact my hound was half wolf made everyone tip-toe when he was near, including the Wagoner's.

As bad as my luck had been of late, I went to sleep on my cot that evening knowing I had been very lucky. I had recovered my money, gotten the dog and the only thing I had not yet attempted to do was recover my horse, saddle, and rifle. It frosted my cookies some that the Starr family had my little sister, but there was little I could do at the moment.

Chapter 8

Gainesville was the county seat for Green County during that era. Paragould was no more than a spot on the edge of a swamp without a name. Some folks were calling it Parmalay. Most settlers in Parmalay chose land up on the ridge, but there were those folks who saw the value in clearing the swamp to the east as well. There were a few shacks scattered about, but it was not a real town. To get anywhere, you still had to go to Gainesville.

Gainesville contained a log hewn courthouse and jail, two stores, four log dwellings and one framed house where the judge lived. Otherwise the population of Greene County was scattered about both sides of Crowley's Ridge.

From 1861 through 1865 progress in Gainesville was arrested as the war took precedence over any planned prosperity. Planned churches, schools and new homes remained abandoned until after the war. All Federal services ceased. The post office was closed down and service was not restored until 1866. Gainesville was the only town in Greene County for over forty years and because of fate, never grew to become a major city.

I found myself at the Depot in Gainesville waiting on the train. I had my father's money and I was not sure where I was headed. You see, most of my father's money was Confederate notes drawn on southern banks, and according to Mr. Wagoner I had to get the paper converted before it was worthless. Vicksburg was under siege, effectively cutting off the east-west supply line for

the southern states. The southern gold coins were fine, because gold is gold no matter how you stamp it, but the south had little in gold coinage.

While I knew the south had fighting spirit, I was losing faith in their ability to win the war, and if the south lost, my money wouldn't be worth the paper it was printed on. A little over seven thousand dollars would be lost unless I listened to how Clifton Wagoner had laid things out for me.

I had a thousand dollars in gold money and I left that with Aunt Sophie. I knew she wasn't my aunt, she was Terri's aunt, but I couldn't help calling her Aunt Sophie, because she treated me like family. My own aunts were scattered all over Arkansas, Missouri and Texas. I hadn't seen any of them in years. Not that I wouldn't like to, but life just hadn't presented me the opportunity.

Unexpectedly I heard a whistle blow in the distance and I knew the St. Louis & Iron Mountain Southern afternoon train was coming in. I was headed back to St. Louis. Nervous, you bet. You'd be nervous going back to a town where the last time you walked the streets you were kidnapped by a slave trader, but St. Louis was the port of entry for everyone going west, and it was the only city nearby where a man or boy could exchange the kind of money I had to exchange. My only hope lay in St Louis.

I'd have to ride all night through the hills to get there, but in the morning if all went well I could make the switch and get out of town on the afternoon train. I know I was hoping for a lot, but you never know what is possible until you try.

Mr. Wagoner had placed all my money in a tightly packed money belt and instructed me on how to cover it

so that no one would know I was carrying anything. I had the belt tight around my waist and so far no one had noticed. Out of necessity he had punched an extra hole in his personal money belt with his leather punch so that it would fit my smaller proportions. I didn't plan on undoing his handiwork until I was standing inside the bank in St. Louis.

When the train pulled into the depot at Gainesville, I handed the conductor my freshly purchased ticket and he ushered me onto the train. I watched up and down the track, and observed another man boarding the train near the rear. Besides me he was the only new passenger. As soon as the train finished taking on water from the water tower, everyone jerked backward, then forward in their seat and the train was under way. I had never ridden a locomotive before, and the experience was an eye opener. If a man wanted to get somewhere, a train was the way to go.

On good days the train could make five hundred miles, on a bad day she still made two hundred or more. A man couldn't do that on a horse even if it had a set of wings.

After a while the sun went down and the St. Louis & Iron Mountain line sped on through the night. I went to sleep by the glow of the dangling lanterns in the passenger car. At times I smelled ladies perfume or tobacco when one of the men in the car would light a pipe or a cigar, but the aroma seemed a comfort to me. The ride was loud, but after a while the drum of the wheels against the steel rails lulled me to sleep.

I heard the whistle blow and the conductor yelled, "Union Station, St. Louis!"

I looked out my window to see the gaslights of the city still glowing in the darkness of the wee morning hours. I did not have fond memories of St. Louis, yet I could not allow one bad experience to determine my future where this city was concerned. No doubt most folks were still in bed, but I had an idea where to get a meal so when I stepped off of the train I headed down toward the wharf. My ticket was a round trip ticket so I held onto my stub and shoved it all into my vest pocket.

I wasn't carrying any luggage and I didn't need any. I did however have my gun strapped around my middle. Anyone bothering me on this day was likely going to get a gun barrel over the head or a bullet in his brisket.

Soon I saw what I was looking for, but the place was not as nice as I remembered. Still, there just wasn't anywhere else to get a good breakfast in St. Louis this early in the morning which I judged to be a little before five. I walked in and shuffled past all the tables to saddle up to the bar. This early in the morning most of the chairs still rested on the tops of the tables so that the floor could be cleaned during the night.

"Hot coffee and a breakfast," I ordered placing my right boot on the brass foot railing next to an old spittoon.

Surveying the room about me was simple as there were only three people in the diner, the cook, the waiter and one man sitting back in the corner of the room half asleep. He seemed to rise a little on my placement of an order, but went right back to half sleeping. It was the man who had gotten on the train in Gainesville same as me.

One thing I knew about St. Louis, there was safety in numbers and soon the old Waterfront café would be full of folks eating breakfast, getting and spreading the news

of the day. That would have to do me until the banks opened up. I didn't know how many of them I might have to visit, but I was intent upon getting my money changed into Yankee greenbacks before the sun set.

St. Louis was mostly dirt streets, some cobblestone and the entire wharf had been converted to a landing for riverboats, a landing made of cobblestone bricks placed tightly together one next to another and logs set deep into sandstone for proper mooring. In my estimation it took real men to place such bricks together and make them stay for many years, but such builders were scarce now that the war had up a full head of steam.

I noticed the man in the corner kept staring at me as I stood next to the bar, and late at night this was a bar or a saloon, but most of the day the Waterfront café was a good place to get a meal. In fact a meal could be had morning, noon or night. I remembered the place when it was in better shape, but the keepers had seen more than one brawl spill out into the street and the wear was beginning to show on the old building. I remembered the place because it sat directly across from the Soulard Market. The market was a tall brick affair which ran the length of two full city blocks and always offered a place for farmers to sell their goods rain or shine. In fact my breakfast likely had its origins from the market across the street.

I had eaten a few meals here in days past, but not one person did I recognize on this morning. The smell of rain was in the air although I hadn't noticed any mud in the town as of yet, but when the lady sat my coffee down on the bar in front of me, it began to pour and thunder rolled rattling the large plate glass window in front.

"Well, that does it," she said. "We're going to have a mess in here today."

The short lady wore her gray hair up in braids. She was wearing a lavender dress which swished as she turned and went back into the kitchen to say something to the cook, but by then all I heard was the rain pouring hard on the tin roof.

She was right, of course, I had seen St. Louis in the rain and the amount of mud that stuck to a man's boots and the wheels of wagons seemed to create a mess of unimaginable proportions. I looked at my boots then which were still clean, but if I ran around town all day looking for a bank to exchange my money, my boots would be wet and muddy. I didn't relish the idea, but there was no getting around the muck.

Presently the gray haired lady returned from the kitchen and placed my plate in front of me. I ate well that morning for the food was good. The eggs were fresh cooked, as was the bacon, and the biscuits were fluffy as well. All of this was topped with gravy which I could not describe other than to say it was about the best I ever had. My coffee was hot.

About that time another character stumbled in out of the rain. I didn't pay him much mind because he was trying to work off a drunk it seemed. At fifteen, food didn't stay on my plate very long. In short order the lady was taking my plate from in front of me.

I glanced over my shoulder at the man who had come in out of the rain. He was starting to snore, chin on his chest. There was no threat perceived by me, so I looked at the other man sitting back in the corner and realized suddenly, he was a threat. The second man was watching

my every move. Here I had a money belt strapped around my middle and my hope was he hadn't seen it, yet the way he was eying me told me different. I was going to have to watch my movements throughout the day to make sure I didn't get ambushed or robbed. His face seemed familiar.

I caught a glimpse of him staring at me more than once as I sipped coffee and waited on the sunrise. Other folks began to wander in and order something to eat while I waited at the bar. What I was afraid of was the fact my money belt might be showing itself around my middle. I couldn't exactly step away from the bar and start tugging on it, for that would be a dead giveaway. I did however manage to glance into the mirror to make sure it wasn't bulging. The best I could tell it seemed out of sight completely.

Aggravation began to settle on me then. When, if ever, was a boy supposed to get an even break? I had business to conduct, and I was minding my own, but for some reason there seemed to be nosey folk's intent upon making my business theirs, whether in St. Louis or back home in Arkansas. Suddenly it dawned upon me—the man who seemed to be watching me was someone I had seen before, but where? I saw him get on the train when I did. Had he followed me all the way from Greene County Arkansas? How did he know this establishment is where I would end up? He had arrived ahead of me.

Finally the sun began to peak over the horizon, but I still had a good wait on my hands. Banks didn't open at sunrise; they had particularly short hours in most cases. The average man worked anywhere from twelve to fourteen hours a day, but banks were open for about six or seven hours only. I figured this was because, if a bank

wasn't open, you couldn't take your money out. Pa always said, "Money goes into those banks, but precious little comes out of them."

I guess that was why Pa preferred to bury his money in mason jars in the yard. There might still be one or two jars left, but I was holding them in the back of my mind just in case the south won the war. One of the best pieces of advice at the time was, "Don't put all of your eggs into one basket." This seemed like good advice to me.

Eventually the hour came when the banks would open and I went out the door. When I looked back over my shoulder there was trouble afoot, because the fellow from the café was coming right along behind me. This forced me to begin wracking my brain, trying to remember where I had seen him before, yet nothing presented itself.

When I got to the first bank they said I might have better luck at Bremmer's bank on Washington Avenue. It so happened that I remembered where that particular institution was so I started in that direction. When I turned the corner I looked back down the street and here the fellow came. I cleared the building and soon as I was out of sight I began to sprint up Washington Avenue which was one of the few streets in town covered in cobblestone brick. Umbrellas were everywhere as the rain continued to come down in buckets; I dodged a few and kept running.

There were people coming and going, but I was light and agile enough to dodge in and out between them. There was nearly three blocks between us when my pursuer turned the corner and realized what I had done. I was looking over my shoulder as he began to run, parting

people as he went. He was a fairly big man, but he had no trouble moving with speed and agility himself. I continued up the small hill, but soon found myself winded.

I bent over to catch my breath and when I looked back he was only a block behind me. Cursing my luck I dove into an alleyway. There simply had to be some way to shake this fellow. Unexpectedly my plans changed. There was a gang of about twenty kids in the alley just ahead of me and they all turned to see me running right at them.

"Well, what do we have here," one of them said.

I stopped in my tracks wondering which was the better bargain, them or the man chasing me. "There's a man chasing me," I shouted.

"What do you want us to do about it?" the oldest boy said.

I didn't wait to answer him, but took off again and tried to run the gauntlet. I was about halfway through them when a boy bigger than me grabbed me by the collar and jerked me off my feet. I jarred the ground as I landed.

"Hold on boy, you can't come through our alley unless you pay us."

I started to answer, but one of them said, "Look Skip, he's wearing a money belt!"

The big boy who had tackled me reached down and jerked my shirt back to look with his own eyes.

"Well I'll be a monkey's uncle," Skip said and reached for the belt.

"Hold up on that shoe shine boys," It was the man who had been chasing me. "Let him up off the ground."

I got to my feet and started to tuck my shirt back in. "Come on over here, Duke."

Well, I looked at the fellow and didn't argue. I stepped around those boys careful like, picking my way through them. As I started to pass Skip, he put his arm up blocking me from going any further.

"You're in our territory mister, and so is Duke as you call him, so you owe us. You two ain't getting off scott free."

That fellow pulled back his trench coat and lifted a dragoon revolver from his holster. He pointed the weapon directly at the boy beside me, I know because I was almost looking down the barrel my own self.

"Now, come on over here, Duke. Otherwise I'm going to have to shoot multiple children and that won't set very well with my morning coffee."

I stepped over to where he stood, wondering all the while how he knew my name.

"You boys see to it you mind your own business and we'll not bother you anymore." Without saying anything else he holstered his gun and we started up the alley. Neither of us said a word for we waited to hear the footsteps coming if they decided to chase us. It was still raining lightly and the sky was a full gray now. The clouds had moved onto the east and covered the city is a gray shroud with fog settling in from the river.

As we neared Bremmer's bank, the fellow stopped us. "My name is Jesse Bowlin, Captain Nathanial Bowlin is my brother. He said to make sure and keep you in one piece. Not too many young folks impress my brother, but somehow you have managed to do exactly that very thing."

It dawned on me then where I had seen him before. That evening they had camped on the old home place this man had been the one setting up to the fire pouring fresh coffee as fast as he could brew it.

"Why would Captain Bowlin worry or care about me?"

"It's like this, Duke. Nathan had been tipped off a few years ago that you father was coming to join his outfit, so he waited on him. Knowing the kind of man your father was, the Ol' Swamp Fox wanted him in our unit, but for some reason your father never showed up. There were rumors here and there about him being kidnapped or bushwhacked, and none of them were pretty, so when he met you he knew exactly who you were. He feels put out about what became of you father, so he told me to watch your back when he learned you were dealing with Captain Franklyn Starr. If you got into any trouble, I was to pull you out. Of course, he never said you might go gallivanting all across the country."

"Thanks, but Pa is dead.

"How do you know?"

"I just buried him last week. Franklyn Starr had something to do with him being shanghaied and Pa told me it was Captain Starr who shot him once he escaped the ship."

"You mean to tell me he was alive and well until last week?" Bowlin asked as we walked.

"Yes sir, he was alive. Not so well since he'd been shot twice, but he was still breathing when I found him."

"You said shanghaied? Where's he been these last two or three years?"

"He was forced to sail the seven seas. I believe Captain Starr was behind that, too. He sure enough shot him when he got near home."

"Nathan says the Starr family is trouble for anyone who comes into contact with them."

"I can vouch for that. I've been fighting with the Starr bunch my entire life with no letup in sight. In fact they have my little sister as we speak, and I don't like it none."

"How did they come by her?"

"I don't rightly know," I said looking over my shoulder. "They may have adopted her. If so, there is little I can do."

As we went up the steps to Bremmer's bank on Washington Avenue, we witnessed the teller opening the door for business and we stepped in. My friend stayed by my side and I was glad of it. I didn't know where to begin, what to say or anything after the morning I'd just had. He did.

"The young man wants to trade some currency," Bowlin ordered.

"Into what?" the teller asked as he opened his window.

"He wants one half in Federal notes and one half converted to French currency, which of course will remain in your bank. Show the man your money, Duke."

I wasn't sure what all that meant, but I didn't hesitate to unstrap my money belt. I laid it on the counter in front of him, and the teller, a Mr. Baum began to count it out. There were a couple of notes he wouldn't honor, because the banks had folded or were in receivership, but I still had six thousand eight hundred and thirty-five dollars he did honor.

You see, before the war started bank notes drawn on individual banks like the Dixie Trust or the Birmingham Savings & Loan, were Confederate money and not as universal as the Yankee greenback. It was worth just as much, there was however no universal note to represent five dollars from any given bank. This, more than anything, was the trouble with southern commerce.

When the teller was finished he counted one hundred dollars to me and the rest we left in his bank. It seemed to me that so far Pa had been right. Money comes in, but not much goes out. I had doubts piling up in my head as we walked out the front door and I said as much.

"Duke, if you were to get robbed like you almost did this morning, you'll thank your lucky stars that the bulk of your money is in that bank. Those drafts you have are good anywhere there's a bank, but they're no good without your signature. You did good, you'll see."

"Some of the Confederate money I still have because it's no good. What's to say that the Yankee greenbacks don't end up being the same way?"

"It will all depend on how the war turns out, Duke. That's why we converted half of your money into French Lira. No matter who wins, you can convert it back when the war is over. For now half of your money is safer as a foreign currency."

"I would have never thought of that."

"That's why Nathan sent me. He knows I can handle this sort of thing to your best interest."

"I'll have to remember to thank him when I get back."

"Nathan is a good man. He has three hundred riders at his beck and call. Whether he needs ten or three hundred, he can round them up in about three hours.

Otherwise they don't exist. That's why the Federals have such a hard time catching anyone. They just go home and resume work on their homesteads. When they break up after a skirmish, there's no tracking them unless you're prepared to send your soldiers to the four winds, and such a decision would be a disaster for any Yankee commander. They would be picked off one at a time. No officer in his right mind will give chase."

We were strolling back toward the train station where we could catch the St. Louis & Iron Mountain Southern back to Arkansas. I was thankful to have such a man willing to advise me, but I was also skeptical. I wasn't used to having folks care much about what happened to Duke John Robinson. This led to my unfounded suspicion more than anything.

At the station we didn't have long to wait. The train would be leaving in about thirty minutes. We took a seat on the depot bench and talked some more. Jesse Bowlin was an educated man, I could tell by the way he talked, which led me to ask a simple question.

"Why do you live in Arkansas?"

"Everybody has to live somewhere, Duke."

"Yeah, I get that, but why Arkansas?"

"Arkansas is as good as anywhere to me."

"I have lived in Arkansas my whole life, but I haven't seen much."

"Depends on what you're looking at. Some men don't need much to survive; others need a whole heaping lot of the unnecessary."

"I never thought too much about life lately, I've been too busy trying to stay alive."

"When you get past the staying alive part, life gets really good."

"I sure hope you're right. I could use a *good* portion considering my circumstance of late."

"Remember this, Duke, rainy days are holidays from God. No one works them. It's a day off for laziness most of the time, but when the rain clears a man better be ready to go back to work."

"You're right, but I never really thought about it before. Rainy days are necessarily kind of lazy."

"It'll likely be raining on us a lot these next few weeks. Won't be much work going on. If you don't mind, I'd like to ride with you. Help you steer clear of any trouble. You've heard the old saying, "an idle mind is the devil's playground."

"My mind is wound up all the time wondering what I need to do next, what will be the most beneficial move, what's right or what's wrong in a given circumstance. There's little chance Ol' Slue-foot can get a hook into me."

"That's good to hear. I wish I had been more like you, but I had to get myself into some of that trouble when I was younger before I realized I had made some wrong decisions. I turned things around, and changed how I got through my days. Sounds like you're on the right track, but you still have to be on the lookout. Ol' Slue-foot is quite an advisory. If you let your guard down, he'll get you right when you're not looking."

The train whistle blew in the distance and we watched as she lazily snaked her way down the steel rails into the Union Depot. She came to a noisy, screeching stop and blew her steam right by where we were sitting. It seemed

as if the engine were alive, huffing and puffing awaiting her orders to take off once again.

A conductor stepped down off the train at the first passenger car placed his step at the door and shouted, "All aboard!"

We got up and walked to the train, displayed our tickets and stepped past the conductor into the car. Neither of us had packed any luggage. We took our seats in the second passenger car and waited for the train to leave the station. I felt at ease as the whistle blew again and the conductor yelled, "Last call!"

When the train started moving I closed my eyes for a moment only and when I again opened them, it was dark. Old number forty seven was speeding down the tracks toward home. I glanced at my partner and he was dozing in his seat. I took a look around to make sure no one was a menace to our current situation and went right back to sleep.

Chapter 9

At sunrise the following morning the train pulled into Gainesville right on schedule. We hopped off and headed for the only place in town to get a good breakfast, Osteen's general store. The thing which had me worked up was the fact how a man could get around nowadays. I had just gone to St. Louis and back in just a little over twenty-four hours. Man, that was flying and I believed if a man scheduled his time right he could make the trip in under twenty-four hours. What a way to travel. I said as much to Mr. Bowlin.

"The world is changing. There are those who say man is not far from being able to harness the wind and fly like an eagle. I know sometimes when that train gets to running downhill I wonder if she isn't flying. I've seen balloons sent up to overlook a battlefield and the officer in the balloon will signal his commander what the enemy is up to. When man gets to control the air we breathe, then man will fly."

"I can hardly see myself flying, Mr. Bowlin."

"I'm with you, but there is talk and such talk usually leads to experimentation which leads to new ways of doing things."

"I don't think I'll see any such thing in my lifetime. If man figures out how to fly it will be thousands of years from now," I said.

Mr. Bowling grinned at me. "A few years ago there was no such thing as a train. That didn't take thousands of

years. There are smart men working around the clock to change the world we live in. Some of them will invent the future. I think flight is closer than either of us might think. The Studebaker wagon makers are tinkering around with the idea of a horseless carriage. I've seen the drawings. The south has a submarine which will go completely under water and right through the enemy lines. We don't know who will invent the next big thing, but the world is changing faster than you or I might think."

"I never really thought about it," I said as we entered the general store on Main Street in Gainesville. Sitting at the counter we ordered coffee and breakfast then talked while we waited. Mr. Bowlin was bringing up things I had never considered. It seemed to me progress was something no man could put a lasso on, yet he might do good to be part of.

"When this war is over this country is going to need good men who can dispense justice, solve disputes and keep the peace," Mr. Bowlin took a sip of coffee. Wiping his mouth on his napkin, he went on. "There will be men who won't know any other way but fighting. The longer the war takes, the tougher that job is going to be, no matter which side wins."

"It seems to me some men want war, just so they can use it as cover to steal what other folks have."

"You're right, Duke, and those men will have to be reined in once the war is settled. You would make a good lawman in a few years. I can see it in your eyes."

"I have enough to worry about just finding what's happened to my brothers and sisters."

"We can find out a good deal right here. Judge O'Steen will know the whereabouts of some of them, Gainesville being the county seat and all. There might even be one or two here in town."

I hadn't thought about it much, but Bowlin was right, I didn't have to go gallivanting all over the countryside to find my brothers and sisters, the records were probably right here in Gainesville. "After we've eaten I think I'll ask Judge O'Steen what he knows."

"Now you are on the right track."

About the time I finished my sentence; Sheriff Morris Wright walked in and took a seat. Some folks said his name was Maurice, but Morris was much easier to pronounce so folks just called him Morris Wright. He ordered coffee and a breakfast also, though he had taken residence at a round table near the front window of the store so that he could keep an eye on his town. That's the way he thought of his little community I was sure. He viewed the town of Gainesville as his own, yet it should belong to the people.

I was beginning to learn at my young age how possessive men were or maybe the word was something else. Regardless, there was no doubt that a man living in that day and age made his britches bigger by how much territory he could run roughshod over. For the sheriff, that meant Greene County Arkansas, and that covered the swampland all the way to the Missouri bootheel at the present time.

There was a whole lot of territory in Arkansas which was unsettled, yet folks were moving in and building homesteads. One of them was Nathanial Bowlin's brother and his wife. They had moved down from Stoddard

County Missouri at the start of the war and settled about ten miles east of town. They had them a spot right on the edge of Crowley's Ridge where they could overlook the forest all the way to the Mississippi River on a good clear day. The land along Crowley's Ridge was beautiful, for I had seen it with my own two eyes, but there was trouble brewing, and the sheriff had not liked the younger Bowlin from the git-go.

Howard Freeman was Nathaniel and Jesse Bowlin's brother-in-law. He was much the same stripe as the men who rode with Captain Bowlin on his raids into Missouri to harass the Federal troops gathered there.

While we were eating our breakfast I saw the sheriff stiffen in his chair, then the door opened and young Howard Freeman stepped in and closed the door behind him. For safety sake, or to prevent any misunderstanding he hung his gun on the hat rack at the door and stood his rifle up against the wall right under it. He then removed his jacket and walked over to where the sheriff was eating his breakfast.

As the man neared, Wright jumped up and back, pulled his gun and began shooting without a word being spoken between the two. Freeman went down in a heap on the floor and lay still, moaning for a moment only. Then all breath was gone and he was dead.

"You saw it," the sheriff yelled, "he was coming for me. All I did was defend myself." The acrid smell of gun smoke still lifted from his gun.

Judge John O'Steen stepped into the room and went to look over the dead man. I couldn't quite see what he was doing, but suddenly he produced a knife and lifted it into the air. "He was armed," O'Steen proclaimed.

"He didn't come in here looking to fight," my friend who was now standing over the dead Freeman answered. He parked his guns at the door when he came in. All the man wanted to do was talk."

"He'll have to do his talking from the grave," Judge O'Steen advised. "Sheriff, this is your mess, I expect you'll be cleaning it up."

"I'll get right on it," Sheriff Wright confirmed.

"Nathanial isn't going to like the way this went down," my friend said.

"Nathanial Bowlin is no worry of mine. He doesn't run Greene County, I do," Sheriff Morris said.

"He's your worry now," Jesse Bowlin responded. "He'll consider this murder the way you handled it. He won't deem this a passing thing. He'll be coming for you when the war is over, maybe sooner. If I were you, I'd look at being sheriff somewhere else."

"You saw what happened," Morris argued, "He came right up to my table to confront me and he was armed."

"With an Arkansas toothpick, and he didn't have that in his hand. Nope, I think what happened here was a cold-blooded murder even if you are the sheriff of Greene County. Judge, I thought you were a better man than this," my partner chided. "Come on, Duke, I think we have worn out our welcome. If we're lucky the sheriff won't shoot us in the back on the way out."

Stopping just long enough to retrieve Mr. Freeman's things at the door, we walked outside and pushed our way through the crowd which had gathered on or near the front porch. I didn't recognize it then, but that crowd was all that kept Sheriff Wright from adding two more victims to the Gainesville cemetery that morning.

"What happened?" someone shouted.

"The sheriff murdered Howard Freeman," my friend said, without stopping. We walked all the way to the livery stable where we had our horses and we saddled up. Mr. Bowlin packed up Freeman's belongings and stepped into the saddle watching over his shoulder the entire time. "We're going to have to run for it Duke, and we have to be on the lookout. We were just witnesses to a murder. The sheriff wants everybody to believe what happened here today was a fair fight and it appears he has the judge on his side, but that shooting wasn't fair, it wasn't even close."

"Are you telling me my life's in danger?"

"Yep, that's exactly what I am telling you. Mine is too. If Sheriff Wright lets us live, the killing of Howard Freeman is going to stink for a very long time and the sheriff's name will be the stink all over it."

We left Gainesville on the run headed for Widow Freeman's house. She was going to get the news first hand. I had seen some shady things in my short life, but suddenly I had seen the worst I ever hoped to see. The killing of a man made legal. I also knew, or at least suspected, the court in Gainesville was crooked as a snake. The entire matter had to have been pre-planned and there was a need for witnesses. It was their word against ours. A sheriff and a judge was pretty strong evidence in anyone's book, but to me the men were no better than Franklyn Starr. They were all men of the same stripe, men of position above suspicion and able to stack the deck. What if they were all working together on some big plot which no one knew about? Was such a thing even possible?

My gut feeling was I had stumbled on the answer, but I was left wondering, just what the plot was and what did they expect to gain? I knew little of government affairs. Officials who wrote the law or documents which governed men was not something I knew anything about, but my intuition told me this had to be the direction things were headed. What were they up to? Did their shenanigans have something to do with the war?

Now when we left the store, all we took was Howard Freeman's things so that we could return them to his young widow. What we had no way of knowing was the fact Sheriff Wright and Judge O'Steen had leveled charges against us for stealing from O'Steen's store when all we had taken was Freeman's weapons. A posse was being formed and neither one of us had any idea we had done anything wrong.

We continued toward the west as the sun began to rise high overhead. Crowley's Ridge was beautiful in these parts, a thing to behold. Mostly a man didn't have to worry about gators this far north, but a few had been known to make their way upstream during the heat of summer months and end up in the swamp bottomland to our east. We crossed the ridge in about three hours and rode into the yard of the man we had just seen murdered a few hours earlier.

As Bowlin stepped down from his horse the front door of the house opened and a pretty lady of about thirty stepped out. "Hi, Trooper Bowlin, what brings you over this way?"

"I have bad news, Martha." The woman's face turned to horror in an instant, her hands went to her mouth and

she almost buckled at the knee. "Your husband has been killed."

When he finished his statement, she did buckle and collapsed on the porch clinging to the hand rail. Suddenly I was remembering Pa. It hadn't been that many days ago I'd buried him at Peach Orchard. As Mrs. Freeman's tears flowed I began to tear up my own self. I suddenly felt all alone, though I knew I was anything but. I had friends and I considered them to be good ones, but what did I know?

Jesse Bowlin sat down on the front porch steps next to Mrs. Freeman and I took the horses to the barn. I unsaddled them and turned them into the corral. The saddles I left in the tack room. I saw there were some oats in the feedbag so a put a few of them out with some hay for the horses. I didn't know how long we might be here, but I could tell you any chance you get to feed a horse a bait of oats, a body should take it, and I took it.

Suddenly the entire world seemed unstable. No one stranger could be trusted in such times as these. Likely as not a young man could be kidnapped and sold into slavery in the blink of an eye. In fact that very thing had almost happened to me not that long ago. If not for Captain Grimes the Confederate Mail Runner for the South I would, myself, be serving aboard ship somewhere on the seven seas.[2] Funny, they had gotten their hands on my father, but I had escaped.

What good was freedom if a man had to defend his very existence every day of his life? The whole thing didn't make a bit of sense to me. Lincoln only delivered his

---

2 Ol' Slantface Mockingbird Lane Press 2014

Emancipation Proclamation a few weeks ago and suddenly the purpose for the war seemed to be shifting to whether or not all men should be free. That wasn't the way things had started out. The rules of war were changing as the thing went along, for better or worse was anyone's guess. I couldn't make heads or tails of the mess myself, but there seemed to be way too much larceny afoot of late. A man couldn't lay his head anywhere safely for any one evening without the worry of losing it before morning.

War can be unnerving in that respect. It takes years to recover from such an unstable environment, years of a young man's life which he would rather not spend in such a way, but wars are wars and what they do to soldiers and civilians alike is never a pretty thing.

My pa once said, "The fountain of youth rides upon the crest of knowledge, the ability to learn from your mistakes and a childish desire to experience every new day as if it is your first." I'm still not sure what he meant when he told me that, but I did memorize it. I have turned it over in my head many times, but for some reason I still did not fully understand the meaning as of yet, of this I was certain.

I liked to memorize things. Sooner or later you could sort out certain quotes, but if you didn't have them memorized, you would never sort them out. At least that's what I believed. I had plenty of sayings in my head to help me sort life out, but I wasn't sure just how they were supposed to help me. Of course I had more learning to do, and in time I would eventually understand all of them, I just didn't know how yet.

One of the sayings was simple; "A gun is neither good nor evil, but a human being makes it so." I can tell you this is correct. Like the gun which killed Captain Bowlin's brother-in-law, I figured was evil. Normally a sheriff's gun was a good thing. I still had a lot to learn in this department, but I at least had a head start where guns were concerned.

"All men are created equal," Pa said, "that ends at birth."

Another quote I had memorized was, "I love the South, a man can still get away with telling the truth in the South!"

Then there was the one which seemed to haunt me all my life, "When you find yourself cursed by both God and Devil it is important to remember; God is the only one willing to help remove the curse."

So, I had met Jesse Bowlin and that was how we began our acquaintance, on a trail which wouldn't see an end for a very long time. At least that was what I thought that day. It's funny how life can change on a moment's notice.

Chapter 10

For the last few years I had been getting by without Pa. As I watched Jesse comfort Freeman's wife on the front porch I sat down on the corral fence and harnessed my own thoughts. What could I do?

Pa had always been part of my life, but like mother he was gone. Somehow I had never really worried about him because I just couldn't picture him dead, even when he was missing. He was always there telling me what to do or guiding me along, but now, now I was alone and I knew Pa would never guide me again.

Inside of me there was a terrible feeling, one of betrayal, letting my father down and a sinking feeling. Without my pa what did I have?

Ma had died when I was only nine and I remembered her only as someone warm who held me as a baby. She doted over me when I got hurt or when I was feeling bad, but in my mind I could no longer picture her. She had been a pretty woman. I still had a picture of her somewhere. She died of a fever only a few years after we settled in the De'Laplaine swamp.

It wasn't long before the Freeman kids came out to see what was wrong with their mother and when they found out, I couldn't bear the thought of it all, the crying and wailing going on was more than I wanted to be part of.

Slipping from my perch on the fence I walked out around the barn then into the swamp. I needed some

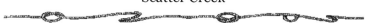

solitude and quiet, some distance between me and what was happening at the Freeman house. I had the idea in my head to go back to town then out to the Wagoner's place at Peach Orchard. I was worried about what would become of my dog, but not much else. If I stopped at the county seat, talking to Judge John Osteen wouldn't do me one bit of good. I was needful to find what had become of my brothers and sisters, but the man would not welcome my presence at this point in time.

After a few hours things had settled down. When I returned Mrs. Freeman had a good meal on. She might have just lost her husband, but she knew there was no lying down on her children. There were plenty of mouths to feed, three little ones no older than five and as I had learned when left in charge of my brothers and sisters, children are always hungry.

We sat up to supper about six that evening but, there was little conversation. No one was saying anything. We just ate a somber meal together. About the time we finished putting away the bulk of our meal, Captain Nathanial Bowlin came riding in with a wagon carrying the body of his brother-in-law. He had with him a force of about twenty men. He was mad, I can tell you that, but he hadn't flown off the handle. He was suddenly cold and calculating. He was also concerned for his brother-in-law's family. Suddenly I realized that Martha was Jesse and Nathaniel Bowlin's sister. Why hadn't it occurred to me before now?

He took us outside away from the family so that he could get our side of what happened in Gainesville. He had heard a version from the Sheriff, and from Judge Osteen, but he didn't believe what they had told him. In

an effort to get the truth Nathaniel Bowlin began to quiz us.

"What happened?"

"The sheriff laid for Howard. He shot him in cold-blood after Howard had discarded his weapons at the front door. It was murder as plain as day, but they held his knife up and claimed he was armed, said he was going to assault the sheriff, but he wasn't about to do no such thing."

"What did he say?"

"That's the thing, he didn't say anything, didn't have a chance to. Sheriff Wright shot him after he laid his guns aside. He didn't have a chance."

I could see the mind of Nathanial Bowlin go from good honest citizen to a man ready to sell his soul to the devil in order to get even for his brother-in-law's death. I saw his eyebrows furrow deeper and deeper as if they took on a life of their own. In an instant he went from a normal sane man to one bent on revenge.

"I'm going to kill him. When I do it will be a fair fight, but I'm going to kill him," Bowlin promised.

"I wouldn't expect anything less from you, Nathan."

Suddenly the past spoke through me. "I have heard that revenge is the lowest form of human behavior on the planet." I don't know why I said it, but it was too late for me to take it back once I had opened my mouth.

"That may well be Duke, but I'm going to kill me a sheriff anyway."

"If you do it, I would sure like to be there to see it," I said.

"When I do," he corrected, "you will be."

Like a sledgehammer the brevity of his words hit me. I had just been drafted, more by circumstance than anything else. I was going to be riding wherever the Swamp Fox went. How else could he make sure I was there when the showdown took place?

I would be learning how to take orders and I would do my best, because as far as I could tell, Captain Nathanial Bowlin was all man. How did a man get to be like him? Suddenly, I wanted to know. He was a legend in these parts, and I can tell you this, Sheriff Wright and Judge O'Steen might wield all the power at the county seat, but they were not comfortable people anymore, no way no how. They had them a king-sized problem and he was better known as Captain Nathaniel Bowlin, the Swamp Fox.

I had heard all of my life, "You become part of what you are around," so I figured hanging around Captain Nathanial Bowlin could only be good for me. These were dark times, with mean men setting out to destroy good people and their families, all for prosperity. I couldn't understand such behavior, but it was obvious some men were unscrupulous in character, willing to slit a child's throat.

We buried Howard Freeman before sunset out at the edge of the swamp. He received a rifle salute and some reading from the Bible. When the affair was over, Captain Bowlin didn't waste a breath. He told us to mount up, all of us, and we hit the trail. He said goodbye to his sister then stepped into his saddle. Leaving two men behind to ensure her safety, he waved his hat and we were off in a cloud of dust.

We headed into the swamp in a northerly direction. This was not the side of Crowley's Ridge which I was familiar with, but I had a pretty good idea where we were. Four miles in we rode into a makeshift campsite where more men were waiting. Stepping down Bowlin gathered his men around the campfire.

"Men, my brother-in-law was killed this morning. From what I gather the shooting was nothing short of cold-blooded murder. I don't want to go into the details, but I want each of you tell me if you hear of anything pertaining to Sheriff Wright. I have a particular interest in seeing justice done in this matter, so anything you hear which concerns the sheriff, I want to know immediately. I don't want anyone else to brace the sheriff or call him out. I'll do that when the time is right."

"In the meantime we will continue our raids. The Yankee's are supposed to be mounting an attack in the swamp area of Northeast Arkansas. I intend to strike them before they reach the St. Francis River. We'll ride out first thing in the morning. I'll post a watch on the island and the rest of us will see if we can't disrupt their plans. Get a good night's rest men, that's an order," he finished.

The following morning we saddled up and headed for Missouri by way of the St. Francis River and Bowlin's Island near Chalk Bluff. The trail was almost the same one I had followed coming home a few weeks earlier. There was not much to eat, but the men seemed to know where they could commandeer a cow before noon so I didn't worry too much about my stomach. On the other hand, I did worry about my position in this company of soldiers. I had no idea what these men expected of me, but I knew

this loose knit assignment wasn't going to be a free ride. There was a war going on and I might be asked to do any number of things up to and including spying on the enemy.

As things turned out spying was my first assignment. I didn't have any experience at being a spy, but Captain Bowlin said I was perfect for the job. I was young enough not to be a suspect, yet smart enough to gather the information he needed. I wasn't so all fired sure, because my stomach was tied in knots by the time I rode into that Yankee camp.

I stepped down from my horse and made my way to the nearest blue belly fire. There was about twenty men spraddled out resting on their saddles as they waited for a slow pot of beans to come to a boil.

"You fella's wouldn't have enough to share with a hungry orphan would you?"

"We got plenty on to boil, for the right kind of chap," the sergeant said.

Well, I knew it was time for my dumbfounded look and that's what I gave him, the dumbest look I could conjure up. I acted as if there was no understanding in me. I looked around at several of the men, sporting my dumb look to see if anyone would help me out. Turns out there was a corporal who wasn't so gung-ho as his sergeant.

"Aw, go easy on him sergeant, can't you see he's hungry?"

"I can see just fine," the sergeant replied. "I'm just wondering what he's doing here?"

"My meals don't come so regular anymore since my pa died," I told him.

"Don't you have a mother," he asked.

"She died several years ago, long before Pa."

"The beans won't be ready for about two hours yet, but you're welcome," he said and turned away. Now that I was welcome, I walked back to Ol' Sho-me and unsaddled my borrowed horse. He looked like he was glad to be done for the day, but my job wouldn't be done until I made my way back to Bowlin's raiders. They were waiting back at the St. Francis River.

I dropped the reigns around a low tree limb and carried my saddle nearer to the fire. I placed it upside down and fell back into it letting my head rest on the soft wool underside. Closing my eyes I thought back to all I had seen. There were about three hundred men in this outfit. I had seen twelve cannons and plenty of cannon balls before I chose my fire. Somehow those cannons needed to be disabled. Suddenly, I wondered how I had managed to get so close without being observed, but my answer came back to me plain—I had been observed.

"Where you from?" The corporal interrupted my thoughts.

The last thing I wanted was to get involved in a conversation with these fellows, but it didn't look like I was going to be able to avoid one. "I was born in Arkansas, but I'm headed for the Rocky Mountains," I said.

"The Rocky Mountains are west."

The way he formed the words, it was an accusation of the first order.

"Yes sir, and the gateway to the west is straight north of here, a place called St. Louis. Anybody wanting to go west should visit St. Louis first. It might save them a whole lot of time and trouble."

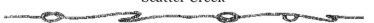

A couple men stretched out around the fire snickered and I was left alone to my thoughts after that. My thoughts were of my friends back at the river. They were ten miles south back at the St. Francis River, putting a lot of faith in me. I didn't have any idea whether I could pull off such a thing as I had been asked to do, but if the captain's plan worked, I could become more valuable to him. I fell asleep along in there and the sergeant had to wake me up so I could eat.

"If you plan on eating, you'd better snap to," he said as he shook my shoulder. He was matter-of-fact when he woke me. I borrowed a spoon and plate then dug in. I didn't want them to think I had lied so I began to show them I had actually been starving. I was in my third plate when the corporal said something.

"Son, you might want to save some for morning, that's breakfast too."

I slowed down then. I made that last plate do a slow dance, but eventually the beans ended up where they ought to be, in my stomach. I cleaned the plate real good down at the creek and handed the field gear back to the soldier I'd borrowed it from.

"It'll be here in the morning whenever you're ready," the fellow said.

"Thanks."

Lying down on my saddle I closed my eyes and tried to gauge the strength of the Yankee unit. I didn't want to befriend these fellows, because my expectations were anyone of them could die once I got back to my unit with the information I was gathering. Still, they were just American's, and for lack of different circumstance I could well be one of these men.

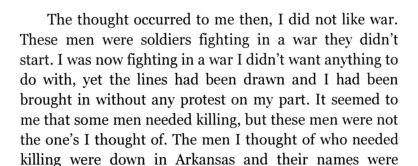

The thought occurred to me then, I did not like war. These men were soldiers fighting in a war they didn't start. I was now fighting in a war I didn't want anything to do with, yet the lines had been drawn and I had been brought in without any protest on my part. It seemed to me that some men needed killing, but these men were not the one's I thought of. The men I thought of who needed killing were down in Arkansas and their names were Wright and Starr.

Had I asked that question out loud with my unit, I could have gotten a dozen Amen and Halleluiah's, but these Yankee's wouldn't have a clue what I was referring to.

Bubba Starr was laid up, at least I had seen to his fate before I volunteered to ride with Captain Bowlin. I had volunteered too. I could have made a good excuse about gathering my brothers and sisters, and he wouldn't have made me ride with him, but I had wanted to. I knew him to be the kind of man Pa would want me to learn from. My brothers and sisters, for the time being, would have to care for themselves.

Captain Bowlin wanted revenge, and although I knew better, I wanted some too. I had been set upon by the Starr family long enough. Not only that, somehow they had my sister, Sarah. She deserved a better home than where she was staying, but how could I make a difference? I hadn't anything to offer her.

The fact that Bubba still had my horse was not lost on me. I was going to get Jericho back sooner or later. I had no intention of letting him go. Bubba had my saddle and rigging, my saddle bags, and my rifle. I wasn't about to let him keep any of it.

I had been responsible for burning down our home, and I felt bad about that now that Pa was gone for good. There I went again, punishing myself for a bad decision, yet how did I know my decision to be bad. Someone might have moved in while I was away, then what? I'd have the exact problem I had tried to avoid. No, my decision had not been a bad decision. The plan had been a good one, only Bubba Starr had disrupted my carefully laid plans.

At some point I had to return to Gainesville and try to locate my family, or what was left of it, because I was the only adult there was left, only I was not an adult in my book at all. I was just trying to survive this crazy circumstance which had been brought on by the war. There were many young boys on both sides fighting, I was no different. It seemed to me we were all too young to be in a war.

Somewhere, I had heard, the Yankee's even had what they called the Orphan Brigade made up of orphans from all around the country. Of all people I knew why they were enlisting. I was one of them. If a boy wanted to eat regular, he joined an army outfit on one side or the other, simple as that. With no home, no father or mother, a boy had to make a decision. While I knew about the Orphan Brigade, I also knew I didn't want to be part of it. Seemed to me that Nathanial Bowlin was a good commander and he was teaching me a lot in a short time.

There was Joker, and I had left him behind on purpose. I didn't want him getting mixed up about where home was, but then I sure hadn't counted on everything that had happened in the last few days either.

A fellow can buy trouble sometimes and not even know he's doing it. I didn't want any more trouble, but

how was I to know when I was planting a seed for it and when I wasn't? That was something I should be asking my father, but he wasn't going to be answering any more questions, not for me or anyone else.

I had my hands full keeping my eyes on these Yankee's for now, so I sobered up and started cataloguing information in my mind, things like troop strength, gun powder, cannons, rifles, six shooters, and so on. They were pretty well armed, but it seemed to me they had a lot of their weapons being worked on at the moment. I made a note of that and fell asleep.

Chapter 11

The following morning I ate a plate of beans and rode out. I had discovered what I wanted to know. I would have to ride to the north and then cut a wide swinging loop around those Yankee's. I rode until I was out of sight and then headed west. Once I had covered about five miles through the rolling hills on Crowley's Ridge I turned south to meet up with my unit.

I had made my error while in the Yankee camp, yet I had not known. It was my eating or lack thereof which had given me away. While I had done a convincing job the night before, I had not thought about playing the part of a starving young man that morning. This led the sergeant to send out a scout and a small patrol to follow me and make sure I was headed north like I said. At some point the patrol got ahead of me and just waited.

When I saw them up ahead I thought it was just a small Yankee patrol scouting the area, but when I got close enough I locked eyes with the corporal who had been at the fire the night before and the yell went up.

"Hold it right there, young man!"

Those words were a signal for me to scat. I didn't try to answer, I didn't step down and I didn't think twice, I slapped spurs to Ol' Sho-me and we took off through the woods up on a high point of Crowley's Ridge. A pistol barked its orders and the bullet tore bark loose from a tree as I dove between two large oaks. I reached up to pull my hat down tighter on my head and that old horse

started running like he knew what a race was for. Small tree limbs leaped out at me trying their best to scratch and scar my face as my horse ploughed through them. He was cutting a trail into deeper forest growth and I let him have his head.

After a minute an open meadow appeared and I put the spurs to Sho-me once again, slapping him on the rump with the reigns. I had to reach the other side of that meadow before those soldiers emerged from the woods. As Ol' Sho-me neared the other side I glanced back and there was no one. I looked back to the front and guided my horse into the best possible opening then ducked. I almost lost my head on a low hanging limb.

Just as we entered the woods on the other side of the meadow the soldiers emerged and began spanking their horses. They had seen me. In another thirty seconds I would have been gone and they would have been slowed, forced to follow the trail on the ground. For the time being they still had a line of sight on me. That was something I wished to change.

There were five men in the patrol and I had seen most of them the night before, especially the corporal who had taken up for me. Now they were after me and my spy gig was up. They knew I was a spy. The question was, did they know where I was headed?

With each stride I was drawing closer and closer to my unit and Captain Nathanial Bowlin. Would they be ready for us? If not, they quickly would be. I was only a few miles from the St. Francis River and I knew the men were there. They were waiting on me. How would Captain Bowlin feel about me bringing a patrol back with me? I could already hear him yelling.

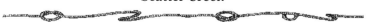

When I rounded the bend which started me downhill toward camp the men came into view. They were cleaning up from breakfast it seemed. When they looked up and saw me they reacted as one. Dropping their plates they grabbed their shooting irons. The men were well under cover when I rode into camp only I didn't stop there, I jumped over a few campfires, a fallen log, and right into the river where I guided my horse toward Bowlin Island at which point Captain Bowlin would be awaiting my report.

I should admit that Bowlin Island wasn't an island at all, but a parcel of ground nestled between what was almost a complete circle of the river before the river straightened south.

As those Yankee's came swarming down the hill after me, I wondered what would happen next. At that moment our rebel detachment opened fire and five Yankee's landed in a heap on the ground. My friends had let them ride after me until they were so close no one could possibly miss. I felt sorry for the corporal who had defended me the night before, but war had an ugly side.

I swam Sho-me across to the island because I had missed the entry and Captain Bowlin was ready for my report when I hopped down.

"Well, young man, have you a report?"

"Yes sir," I answered.

"Then make it."

"Three hundred Yankee's are camped about ten miles due north of here sir, at least they were last night. They seemed to be waiting on something, orders, ammunition, I'm not sure, but half of their rifles are out of commission being tended to by the gunsmith, and they have twelve

cannons sir, but I didn't see the balls anywhere. There is nothing wrong with their dragoon revolvers."

"What was that shooting across the river?"

"A Yankee patrol had seen me and tried to stop me, sir. I think they rode into an ambush, the same lines I just rode through."

"You see that Jesse?" Bowlin turned to his brother standing behind him. "That's why I told you to mentor this boy, he's good. He was better on his first trip than my most experienced scouts."

Well, I can't tell you the pride which was welling up in me. I was getting a pat on the back for my work. Something I was not at all used to. Bowlin didn't say anything else, but he was doing some thinking. Without taking his attention off the problem at hand, Captain Nathanial Bowlin began to shout orders to his men, his eyes on me the whole time. This left me intimidated in such a way I took a step back.

"I'm not through with you, Duke, just hold on," and his orders continued.

He finished barking orders to the rest of his officers which were on the island then stared at me for a long minute and said, "Duke, when we move out I want you beside me on my right flank. You stay there until I tell you different, do you understand?"

"Yes sir," I responded.

"Good, now take care of your horse because, his rest will be short."

I didn't unsaddle him because Bowlin had just ordered everyone to get ready for an engagement. That meant we would be moving out soon. Several of the subordinate officers were already in the water headed for

their men. Bowlin's orders were being carried out and we would soon be under way.

It occurred to me that Nathanial Bowlin had forgotten about his dead brother-in-law already.

"I know what you're thinking. What about my brother-in-law? It was as if the captain had read my mind. "Duke, there is a time and a season for everything in this life and right now there's a war going on. Howard's justice can wait. In fact, what I have to do will be easier if I let Sheriff Wright stew on what he's done for a while. He might just forget I'm out here and let his guard down, or his guilt will eat him up. Anyway, it isn't time," he informed me.

"Yes sir," I said and led my horse to the water's edge.

I let Ol' Sho-me drink his fill and crop grass for about two minutes. He was thankful for the little he got and then I stepped into the saddle seeing Nathanial Bowlin was doing the same. We forded the river with me on his right flank. He said he wanted me there and that was where I intended to stay until the Swamp Fox told me different.

When I thought about it, I didn't really know anything about Captain Nathanial Bowlin, but the way he carried himself left no doubt as to who was in charge. He commanded respect wherever he rode, yet he didn't have to say anything. Whether it was his men or some no account drifter, something the war was creating a lot of lately, everyone showed him the same respect. If I didn't know better, I would have assumed the general's worked for him.

As we rode out of the water on the Missouri side, the commander rode up and down his flanks to make sure

everyone was ready. He took a report from Lieutenant Jesse Bowlin who said the Yankee horses had been turned loose on the Arkansas side of the river where their US brand would get them a home soon enough. No one wanted to get caught riding one of those horses in a battle against the Federal troops.

The soldiers were being dug a fair grave and the small detachment was to return home when they were finished, yet there was no time for a marker. I looked down on the corporal and the men from the night before and suddenly I was sick. One of them was the man who had lent me his eating utensils. Jesse's report was noted and we moved out, me on one side and Lieutenant Jesse Bowlin on the other side of the Swamp Fox.

Duke John Robinson was a full-fledged Rebel in the Confederate army just like that. I hadn't wanted any part in the war, all I wanted to do was grow up and that seemed more difficult with each passing day. When war encroaches on a young man's life, it demands your full attention. I was learning that lesson real good.

I was riding north on a raid into Missouri, I still didn't have my horse and I had no idea about my dog. By now the Wagoner's probably suspected me dead. I can tell you this, my life was no longer my own. Funny how that works, I was just an innocent young man trying to survive what everyone else seemed bent on doing to me and here I was riding into battle. Strange how life could come up with a plan like this!

Nathaniel Bowlin took the lead which meant I was riding up front. For the life of me I couldn't see what the Confederate captain saw in me. I was at a loss to explain his faith in someone as young as I. If he knew how many

times I had waltzed head long into trouble, he would no doubt discard me at once. I knew how rocky my road was, did he?

"That card game was impressive. I was sitting across the table from your father when he ran out of money."

"Sir?"

"In Gainesville a couple of weeks ago, I was playing cards with your father, Frank Scott, Richard and Frank Jackson and Captain Starr. Well son, I never saw such a thing in my life, not in all of my born days. When your father raised us that last time he took out his six gun and for a long moment nobody knew if he was fixing to part someone's hair or plug one of us.

"This here revolver ought to be worth twenty-five dollars," he said. "I'll raise you twenty," and he laid it on the table.

"When all was said and done only Captain Starr and Frank Jackson were left in the hand with your pa. I bowed out as did Frank Scott and Richard Jackson. When the showdown came, your father was holding a straight flush to the queen. Well Duke, he won that hand fair and square, put his pistol back in his holster and began to play like a man on fire. He won seven, maybe eight thousand dollars the rest of the evening. I was smart enough to get out, but Starr seemed to have something to prove. He stayed until he bet the farm. He had been losing steadily for hours and had nothing left, so he bet the homestead he has in the De'Laplaine swamp. He lost."

"I don't understand, sir."

"He lost his home, he lost everything to your father, and was I a betting man, and I am, I bet he laid for your pa in the swamp when he headed home."

We rode north, but my mind was somewhere else altogether. Franklyn Starr had killed my pa in order to get the deed to his land back! He took the money Pa had won too. Just when, if ever, would the Starr family stop setting on people and doing them wrong? If I hadn't trouble with them before, I sure as dickens had something to settle now. Franklyn Starr had killed my pa, and now I knew why, partly because he hadn't stayed away, and partly because Pa got the better of him in a poker game on his return. It seemed to me the better man was gone.

"Duke, I told you that so that you would know the full story about what happened to your father. Now, we have a battle to wage, and I expect you don't want to get yourself killed with your thoughts somewhere else, so focus on what we're about to do. You'll get your turn with Captain Starr later. You ride with me, and I'll see to it."

I thought about what he said to me and figured he was probably right. He had a score to settle with the sheriff at Gainesville, so if he could wait, so could Duke John Robinson. I settled in then and began to listen, paying attention to what was happening around me. If I got my head blown off now I would never get the chance to take care of Captain Starr like I wanted, not to mention Bubba. The pair had been a thorn in my side for years and it was my intention to remove that thorn once and for all.

Chapter 12

You just don't know what life has in store for you until you saddle up. We caught those Yankee's flatfooted, mostly unarmed and nowhere near ready for a fight. When Captain Bowlin yelled charge, seventy-five men rushed through the Yankee camp shooting and hurrahing anything that moved. They had seen us coming, but most of their weapons were at the forge being repaired. A few of the men had guns handy, but as a whole, the soldiers were unarmed, their weapons stacked near a camp fire.

When we gathered three miles north of the skirmish, many of the Union horses had broken free and ran with us. Gathering them up, we turned west for about five miles and then headed back into the swamps of Northeast Arkansas. We passed our camp site from the previous day and headed south. That evening we camped on the edge of the Pfeiffer farm which was about seventeen miles south along Crowley's Ridge. Captain Bowlin traded some of the Union stock and the next morning we all disbanded to head for home.

I shadowed Jesse Bowlin and his friend, but when we rode into the yard at his house there was trouble afoot. Remember I mentioned that the sheriff had gathered up a posse to go after us? This was the morning I actually learned about the posse. They rode into the yard about ten minutes after we did. There wasn't much talking to do because guns started going off around me before I had any idea that we had company.

I saw Jesse go down and then Sheriff Wright rode over to where he was lying and ordered a slug put in his head. I knew right then I was in more trouble than a boy ought to face. If Sheriff Wright and his posse were willing to commit cold-blooded murder in front of me, I had little chance but to run for my life and that's just what I did. I jumped on the back of Ol' Sho-me and I was away. Bullets searched the air for me, but none of them found their mark. The only good thing to come out of our trip home was the fact that Jesse had taken a couple of the posse with him. He didn't die alone that day.

I knew those posse members to be misled men, but innocence was not a stay of execution where war was concerned and it dawned on me that I was now fighting two wars, one at home and one abroad just like Nathaniel Bowlin. I was part of the travesty about to play out whether I wanted to be or not. The thing what bothered me was; how was I supposed to live through such a tangled up mess? If this was God's plan for my life, just what kind of chance did a boy like me have?

Right then I didn't give myself much of a chance to live through to the end of the war or through the end of the day for that matter. Sheriff Morris Wright wanted me dead and there was a posse breathing down the back of my neck.

I put the spurs to Ol' Sho-me and headed back north with the hope I might run into some of the men from our outfit. When I looked over my shoulder, Zach Holmes was not far behind me. He had been the third man in our party that morning. I slowed up a mite to let him catch up and asked, "Where's the best place to go?"

"Back to the Pfeiffer place, come on!"

I leaned forward in the saddle and we took out figuring the Swamp Fox was our best line of defense. Captain Bowlin's place was up on the St. Frances River not far from Bowlin's Island on the edge of the Arkansas line. One thing I knew for sure, he was going to be hopping mad that the sheriff had killed his brother.

I rode with one thought in mind, staying only one step or two behind Zachery Holmes. He had blood leaking from the back of his flannel shirt as we leaned forward into the wind. I could tell he was struggling to stay in the saddle, but he hung onto his horse as if his life depended on it. There was no trail the direction we took, so we were making one as we went. The swamp seemed always present on our right, but we were up on the ridgeline one minute, down in the swamp bottoms the next.

A log appeared before us and the horse before me jumped the obstacle with ease, yet Zach almost came off. I heard him grunt when the animal came down and I knew he was in real trouble. Ol' Sho-me leaped the fallen log as if born to be a jumper and came down so smooth I hardly noticed a change in his stride. From where we were, I knew there had to be miles of traveling ahead of us, but it couldn't be helped.

We galloped north, looking for anyone we could call friend. Tree limbs and brush slapped at us all the while. There was no trail the way we were headed, but I surmised there should have been. It was fairly even going along the edge of the ridge. For about three hours we rode, and eventually we came to the Pfeiffer Ranch where we could get some help, help which Zach Holmes needed or he was going to die.

As we entered the yard the people in the house seemed to empty out of every door. Before I could say anything about what had happened, several folks whom I could not place, were taking Zach down from his horse. He had lost a lot of blood and I was worried he might die. If he survived, it would be because he didn't give up easily.

"Hop down son, you might as well eat," the oldest man said.

"I've got to get to Captain Bowlin, his brother has been killed."

"Can you do anything to bring him back?"

"Well, no sir, but..."

"Then step down and get some grit in your stomach. Your news can wait ten minutes. Otherwise you might ride yourself to death and be of no good to anybody, not even the captain."

Reaching up the man steadied my horse by grabbing his halter and I stepped down. His argument made good sense, mostly because I was hungry.

"Let your horse be and come on up to the house. Ma just finished cooking and you look as if you could eat."

I did as I was instructed and took my seat at the table. There was a full supper on, but the women were off upstairs somewhere trying to save Zach. Two other young men came in and sat down as the oldest began to thank the Lord for all of us. He said a short prayer for Zach who was in terrible shape and then we all started in to eat.

I didn't know much about the Pfeiffer family, but enough to know they were good folks. We had stopped here on our way south. They had fed us and bought much of the Union stock we had unexpectedly commandeered.

The farm was a real working farm, and the Pfeiffer family grew crops in the lower bottoms, but also up on the ridge. Some crops did better in the flood plains while others needed much less water, both options were good soil. In short, they seemed to know what they were doing.

The meal was chicken and dumplings with cornbread and green beans. I was hungry all right. Hungry enough to eat it all, but I showed some restraint and practiced my manners.

When I was finished old man Pfeiffer leaned back and said, "Now, go on and get yourself killed if'n you so desire, but know this, no man or boy has ever left my home hungry."

I stood up and thanked him. As I took my hat down off the hat rack by the door I realized the only reason he fed me was so that he could still say no man or boy ever left his house hungry. When I got out to my horse my saddle was on a fresh Union mount sporting a US brand. Ol' Sho-me was in the corral where he needed to be. A black boy handed me the reins to my new mount and said, "Your horse needs rest, he'll be ready and grain fed when you get back."

"You speak good English for a colored boy," I observed.

"I was raised by the Pfeiffer family as one of their own. I'm no slave."

I checked to make sure I had my borrowed rifle and I stepped into the saddle. It would take another hour to reach Captain Bowlin, if he was in the area.

"What's your name?" I asked.

"The name is Nikoli Lombard. The folks call me Nick."

"I'll see you, Nick. Thanks for getting the horse ready."

Turning the US Calvary horse toward the north, I put spurs to him and rode out of the yard at full speed. I was in the woods in short order following a trail I had been on before. I knew the cliff was looming ahead of me so I slowed the mount down and made a good turn, then worked my way to the bottom. Once my mount gained his feet on low ground I again put spurs to him. We were running with the wind when I noticed that Captain Bowlin was headed my way with a couple of his men. As I neared their ranks I pulled up short.

"Captain Bowlin, sir, I have news of your brother, Jesse."

"Well, what is it?"

"He's been killed by Sheriff Wright, sir. I saw it happen. The sheriff walked over to where he lay wounded on the ground and ordered his men to shoot him dead. Three different men shot him in the head."

I saw Bowlin's face turn dark once again. This time there seemed to be no recovery for him. His brother had been murdered and he was fuming mad. I understood, because that Starr bunch had killed my own father. I was caught up in an unbelievable mess now. There was no turning back, not for me or for the Confederate soldier known as the Swamp Fox. We were on a collision course with the very law which was supposed to be protecting us. Somebody was going to die, the question was, us or them?

No further words were spoken. I saw a tear develop in Captain Bowlin's left eye then his right as his hate for Sheriff Wright turned into compassion for his dead brother. He did not move for what seemed like hours, but it was only a few minutes.

"Duke John Robinson, you and I are in the same boat paddling upstream. We are fighting evil now, so I want you to side me no matter what happens."

"Yes sir."

"If we end up in a shooting match, it will be us against the Starr family as well as Sheriff Wright. I help you and you help me, get it?"

"Yes sir," I repeated.

"Good."

"Sir?"

"What is it, Duke?"

"Zachery Holmes was seriously wounded. He's at the Pfeiffer Farm."

"I'd like to make my way back to the Pfeiffer place and see how he's coming along."

I turned my Union Calvary horse around and fell into step with the captain and his men. We were headed to a place I considered to be safe. The Pfeiffer farm was one place Sheriff Wright would not go. The old man had run him off more than once at gun point until he no longer wished to travel by way of the farm.

"Boys, I make a pledge to you this day. I'm going to kill me a sheriff, and from what Duke told me I have every right. If any one of you disagrees with me, now is the time for you to ride. I won't hold it against you," he told the other men.

"Well sir, I believe I'll stay," one of the men answered.

The other two followed in agreement. Four men and a boy not yet grown were suddenly on a mission to get even. I didn't know it then, but when a man sets out to get even with someone for the sake of revenge, they're starting down a slippery slope. Revenge is the lowest form of

human behavior on the planet I'd heard tell. I didn't know how bad things could get right then, so I stepped right out onto that slippery slope and almost didn't make it back.

Satan will collect children just like he'll collect grown men, I know that now. It doesn't matter if you're ten or twenty or thirty, he's after you before you even know you're in a game for your life. I don't mind playing games, when the time was appropriate, but I don't like playing games with the Devil. We were doing exactly that. All evidence pointed to the fact he was in Arkansas.

At the Pfeiffer farm we settled down for the evening while Zach still fought for his life. The men were engaged in man talk and I didn't really fit in with their discussion, so I found Nick and we spent a little time getting to know one another. As it turns out, the Pfeiffer farm had been engaged as part of the Underground Railroad for several years prior to the start of the war. Nick's mother had been mortally wounded in her escape and the family adopted him at the age of three. He was now sixteen.

He showed me his mother's grave and the moment was somber. If I wasn't careful I would be sporting one real soon, headstone and all. Suddenly it occurred to me; The Underground Railroad! This was a group of people who smuggled slaves out of the south! Was I missing something? Why was Captain Bowlin friends with these people? I thought the south was fighting for slavery. I said as much to Nick.

"Duke, the south isn't fighting over slavery, they're fighting over taxes that are being imposed on the slaves. The Federal Government now wants to collect taxes on every slave the south owns."

"So they aren't really fighting over slavery?" I asked.

"It is and it isn't. They're fighting over excessive taxes which most folks in the north don't have to pay. Most folks in the south don't have to pay them either. I heard the old man say one time, there are forty-five thousand slave owners in the south, and thirteen million white folks who don't own a single one. He said that's less than one percent of the population."

"How do you know so much?"

"When the old man talks, I listen and I study with the Pfeiffer children. Lincoln didn't even care about the slaves according to the old man. Otherwise he wouldn't have waited until this spring to offer his Emancipation Proclamation. The war started because the Federal Government was swinging too wide a loop wanting to tell the states what to do. The Federal Government was never supposed to be that big or powerful. Mr. Pfeiffer says if the Yankee's win, we'll all become slaves to the Federal Government. We'll be taxed right back into slavery, only everybody will become slaves, not just the blacks."

"And here I thought you weren't worried about how the war turned out."

He hit me then, right in the mouth with everything he had, and his punch had something. I went down in a heap right there by the corral and before I could get up he had me pinned to the ground hitting me some more. I was turning my head with the punches, trying to reduce their sting, but he was having his way while I struggled to dodge even one blow.

Suddenly the men were there pulling him off of me.

"Here now, what's going on here," Mr. Pfeiffer yelled.

"He started it," Nick pointed at me.

"How did I start it?" I struggled to understand.

"He said I didn't care how the war turns out," Nick accused.

"Hold on boys," Mr. Pfeiffer said. "I think I know what's wrong with him. Duke," he said to me, "the boy's mother is buried right there. She died trying to escape slavery. This war has started a lot of hard feelings on both sides. He's not mad about what you think, but you insulted him." Again the man pointed to the grave of Nick's mother.

"I think you can settle this with an apology," Mr. Pfeiffer allowed. "I think this is just a minor misunderstanding."

I looked at the boy long and hard, not sure if I was getting proper advice, but in the end I offered up an apology. "I'm sorry, Nick. I didn't mean any harm. I guess I just didn't understand."

"Well, Nick," Mr. Pfeiffer prodded.

"Apology accepted."

"Now, you boys shake on it."

We shook and the men turned around and went right back to the house. This left me worried about whether or not Nick had been sincere in his handshake. The upshot was, I didn't even know what I had just apologized for, so my gut was telling me something like this might happen again. I shouldn't have been worried at all, but the thing about trouble is; there's usually no warning smell, no warning sign at all, not until after the trouble's happened. In hind sight a man could spot trouble a mile away, but in foresight, it just wasn't possible, or so I thought at the time. I had a heap of learning to do in that department.

"I guess I stepped in it real good," I admitted.

"You sure did," Nick agreed.

"Now what?"

"I say we race to that oak tree over yonder and see who is fastest."

I knew if I had any chance to beat him it would require that I get the jump on him, so I gave the only answer which made sense to me and I took off at a dead run. Nick had been facing me when he pointed to the tree, so I had a good three or four step advantage on him before he knew I was giving him an answer. The thing was, by the time we had taken twenty steps in that direction he passed me by like I was a turtle at the annual turtle races.

He was standing there waiting for me when I came struggling to the tree. I got my bottom handed to me, because once Nick got his legs wound up under him he ran like a deer. There was no way I would ever outrun him unless he was on crutches.

"The girls run faster than you do," he laughed.

I knew exactly who he was talking about. The Pfeiffer's had a few girls about my age and they were in the house most of the time. I didn't like it much, but I took his ribbing, mostly because I didn't want to start another fight.

"You want to catch some lightning bugs?" he asked.

"Some what?"

"You know, fireflies."

"What do I want to do that for?"

"Come on, I'll show you."

We took off up to the house where we got a couple of mason jars and punched tiny holes in the lids to give the flies air. As we were prepping, the two Pfeiffer girls joined in the festivities and when we went out the door the four of us had two jars between us. When the sun is going

down of an evening is the best time to catch the little buggers, and this evening was no exception. The girls were laughing and frolicking, and suddenly I understood why Nick wanted to catch fireflies, he wanted to watch the girls catch them. He was doing very little himself.

I caught on rather quick and soon the girls were running to and fro while the two of us grabbed a lightning bug now and then, just enough to keep up the appearance we were participating, when what we were really doing was watching the girls. I had the thought that Nick had done this many times.

Sooner than I wanted, the girls were called into the house and told to get ready for bed. I was to sleep in the barn along with Captain Bowlin and the men. Nick had his own room in the house along with the rest of the children.

We set about making ourselves comfortable in the hay loft once we were certain there were no snakes to share our beds. In this part of Arkansas, copperheads and water moccasin's were common as were puff adders. I didn't want to cross paths with any one of them, no one did, but every once in a while one of them would just happen to be right where you were.

Just as I was about to spread my blanket roll a puff adder came slithering out from between two bales of hay, the light of the lantern not yet put out, dancing off his colorful back. I yanked my handgun and fired all six shots at the snake, missing every time. That snake danced like he could see the bullets coming out of the end of my gun. Now he was mad, his neck spread wide like a cobra.

I was about to turn and run when Captain Bowlin blew him into the next county with a blast from his shotgun.

"You got to use the right weapon, Duke."

I suddenly knew that a shotgun was the right weapon for any snake, simply because there was nothing left to pick up. The snake had disappeared in the blink of an eye. Look though I may, I didn't find enough of that snake to even know it was ever there. A piece of bloody meat about one inch in diameter is all I found.

"Everything all right out here?" It was Mr. Pfeiffer at the barn door.

"Yep, Duke had a bed partner he didn't want, a puff adder," Captain Bowlin stated.

"I thought maybe the war had found its way into my barn."

"Nope, we'll be all right now." Captain Bowlin smiled as he put out the lantern.

With that Mr. Pfeiffer closed the door and we men got some rest, everyone but me. I couldn't sleep a wink because of that snake. I kept wondering where the next one was. While the men I rode with snored away, I picked up my things and climbed down the ladder to what I was certain meant safety. I had to get some distance between me and that dead snake, the one I couldn't find.

Putting my blanket on the front porch swing I snuggled in for the night. I didn't figure to find any snake on the Pfeiffer's front porch swing. In no time I had thoughts running through my head, thoughts of what was to become of me. What might be the fate of Duke John Robinson? If I could survive this crazy war, what then? I had planned to go west, but that was now on hold.

Somewhere along in there I fell asleep, only to be awakened for breakfast just before sunup the following morning.

Chapter 13

At breakfast most of the fun was at my expense. There were more jokes told on me that morning than I'd had leveled my way in fifteen years. I couldn't hit the broad side of a barn. My bullets were designed to seek out anything but a target, scared of snakes and so on. I took it, not minding at all. I deserved some of it, and none of the puns were really insulting, just the fellows trying to laugh, we all needed a good laugh back then.

After breakfast we rode out and headed for the county seat known as Gainesville. I figured we were about to have it out with the sheriff. In my youthful mind there could be no other reason, but I learned different as two more of Bowlin's riders soon appeared beside us.

John Stone was one of the men who rode up. He was a well-kept man, but he wore a long black beard and his side arm was a silver plated long nose Smith and Wesson.

"John, you figure you can set the courthouse up in flames where the town can't save it?" Captain Bowlin asked.

"What are you figuring on?"

"They'll be writing up legal documents to account for their actions of late, legal documents which will be nothing but a fraudulent representation of the facts. I don't want them to ever be public record. If they were true, I wouldn't mind, but you know as well as I do that anything the sheriff says about what happened will be a total lie."

"Why, it would be my pleasure, captain. We'll need some kerosene though."

"We can get that easy."

We rode on then and I knew we weren't riding into a gunfight, but an arson attempt, and you know what? I was glad. I felt like I was on the right side, even though I was running afoul of the law in these parts. Of course, I knew what to expect to a degree, as memories returned of me burning down our house at De'Laplaine

There's man's law, and then there is God's law. A man what won't follow God's law has little hope of following manmade laws. As such, Sheriff Wright was all the proof I needed. In my previous experience there was the preacher Jeremiah Culpepper and Ol' Slantface as well, but Sheriff Wright had a unique and special understanding of the law, none of which applied directly to him.

As I thought about Ol' Slantface, I wondered how he and Dillon Childs were getting along. The last I'd heard those two had taken off to run down the preacher after being laid up at Reelfoot Lake for a spell. The preacher had ambushed them and went after a gold shipment intended to buy supplies for the south. Myself and Rassie Cohen had acquired horses for the two while they lay in bed recovering from gunshot wounds, courtesy of the preacher Jeremiah Culpepper.[3]

Had they caught the preacher man? He was a bad one. I wasn't betting on it. If they did catch up, taking him would not be easy. I had a good recollection of him and Ol' Slantface, having been kidnapped off the streets of St. Louis, and I was not positive they could catch the man or

---

3 Ol' Slantface Mockingbird Lane Press 2014

stop him from stealing the gold shipment. Jeremiah Culpepper would take a whole lot of killing if I was right. My thoughts went wild then, just wondering what might happen when Dillon and Ol' Slantface caught up with the evil preacher from Black Creek.

We stopped at a small abandoned cabin where John Stone gathered the necessary fuel to burn down the entire Greene County Courthouse and do a thorough job, grabbing up a dozen sticks of dynamite for extra measure. We set up right there for lunch and waited till near night fall before saddling up again.

I listened as the men talked of this friend or that which had joined the Arkansas 5th, a unit which had earned the nickname "The Fighting Fifth." Those men were over in Tennessee near Chattanooga holding a ridge overlooking the town, something called Chickamauga. Three had come back to Gainesville in pine boxes on the train a few weeks ago.

Finally as the sun dipped low in the west we saddled up to ride. The closer to town we got the more the men grew silent. It was dark now and we would be entering town from the north which required riding by the coffin store of J. Nutt who was doing a brisk business of late. We rode past the coffin store then right down Main Street past the Frank Scott store, Dr. Gregory's office, the Morhill Bakery and Early's store. Turning west between Early's store and Dr. Graham and Dr. Hopkins office we made our way to the back and crossed Scatter Creek Road just east of the bridge to the courthouse which wasn't much, just a two room building set apart from the rest of the town looking almost like a church and probably had been at one time.

Captain Bowlin gave me a container of kerosene and told me how and where to pour it, the other men already seemed to know what to do. I did too, but I wasn't about to let on that I had experience in such matters. Then taking the dynamite from his pocket, John Stone tossed the sticks into an open window. This was good luck because usually all of the windows were locked shut, but on this night someone had missed one or left it open on purpose. As things stood, we didn't have to break any glass or make a bunch of noise to place the explosives.

When we were finished we stepped into the saddle and eased out of town the way we had come leaving John Stone alone to light the courthouse on fire. He made sure we were well away before we saw the night sky light up. The courthouse was burning no question about it. Without warning there was a loud explosion. With no more windows to stop the air from getting inside the courthouse, it went up in flames almost instantly. There would be no stopping such a fire with all the windows blown out. A few moments later as we looked on we saw the small dome roof collapse.

Presently John Stone came riding into view walking his horse as if there wasn't any urgency. This surprised me, but when he saw the quizzical look on my face, he smiled.

"If I had run my horse folks in town would have known instantly which way I went. I would have brought them right to you."

Turning his horse around we sat there on the road and watched the commotion in town. Folks were running, yelling and screaming, throwing buckets of water on the building, water which evaporated instantly. There was no

stopping such a fire. The jail house had been right next door, but far enough away prisoners wouldn't get caught up in the flames.

"How did you get away without being seen," I asked.

"I was in Scatter Creek when I lit the building on fire. I was low enough down no one saw me, so I left by the shadow of the creek."

"Let's get out of here before someone accidently stumbles on us," Captain Bowlin suggested. "They obviously won't be able to save anything in the way of records or documents."

We turned our horses to the north and made our way back to the Jesse Bowlin cabin where we stayed the night. Jesse's wife had stayed in Missouri with her parents when Jesse came to Arkansas just before the war. A good thing I was certain, because I had the suspicion if she'd been here when Jesse was killed, Sheriff Wright would have killed her too.

In Greene County of late, it was getting so that every citizen went armed, man or woman, it didn't matter. All were becoming afraid of the sheriff who was getting too big for his britches. It was getting so that good decent folks were afraid to do their chores outside, afraid they might run into a grouch of a sheriff who would shoot first and then not even ask questions.

He was terrorizing the county's citizens, and from what I could tell, he didn't have to answer to anyone. Gainesville was so far from anywhere that Sheriff Wright was able to do as he pleased, much to the dismay of the community. With the war on, there just wasn't anyone at the state capitol who cared about what happened in Greene County Arkansas.

More than one letter had been addressed to the state capitol about the aggressive nature of the sheriff toward the citizens, but no one seemed to care, if they did they sure had a funny way of showing it. There had been nary a response concerning the heavy handed ways of Sheriff Wright.

The following morning we had a hasty breakfast then saddled up to ride. There was no question where we were riding, the Pfeiffer farm to check on Zach Holmes. I rode with Captain Bowlin, John Stone, Bob Eubanks, Emile Haynes, Vern Truman and Wade Farley. This fact put my mind at ease because each man was quite capable on his own, but not completely, as Sheriff Wright had become an extremely unpleasant sort of man lately.

Wright had on many occasions used his firearms when he could have avoided a conflict altogether. He was becoming a holy terror, known to be reckless, dangerous and unscrupulous. Wright had several times communicated to Captain Bowlin that he would kill him.

We took no trail the following morning. If Sheriff Wright was going to apprehend the culprits who burned down the courthouse, he was going to have to track us down. We turned east into the swamp at the edge of Crowley's Ridge and then turned north. Several times we crossed the direct path Zack and I had taken to reach the Pfeiffer farm, but we never stayed on the trail. We rode deep into the swamp at times, but never up on the ridge until we were near the farm.

After about three hours riding in all sort of swamp conditions, Captain Bowlin brought everyone to a halt and issued the signal for quiet. We could hear them in the

woods ahead of us, if it was Sheriff Wright, he and his posse were making enough noise to wake the dead.

We sat in silence as the detachment of men argued and fussed over which way to go. Finally they picked a direction and headed west toward Crowley's Ridge. Waiting about ten minutes, Captain Bowlin waved for us to move on. When we reached the spot where the men had been Bowlin began looking over their tracks. "Wade, you're the tracker, what do you think?"

"Lost soldier boys, Union, and it looks like they just want to find a way out of the swamp."

"What are they doing in the swamps down here?"

"Looking for you more than likely captain, you and us," Wade reasoned.

"Well, they darn near found us."

"Darn near don't get the job done captain."

"Shall we follow them?" John Stone asked.

"I think we shall," Bowlin affirmed. "How many you figure Wade?"

"About ten the best I can tell."

"What would happen if we led those men directly to Sheriff Wright?"

John Stone cleared his throat and a big smile appeared on his face. "Well captain, we might be rid of a Yankee detachment, but we might be rid of the county sheriff."

"That's exactly what I was thinking. Wade, you take the point," Bowlin commanded.

Wade Farley fell into the tracks which led off in the direction of Crowley's Ridge and we fell directly in line behind him, following a squad of Yankee soldier boys. The way Captain Bowlin's mind worked when there was battle

to be fought was something to witness. He had ways of making things happen which most people didn't have any idea about. I was getting a first class education in tactics, but I wasn't the only one.

We held back about fifty yards behind Farley while he sorted out the trail. This was slow going in the swamp, but those men left a trail behind, and Farley was more than capable of tracking them. I had tracked a big boar one time, an Arkansas Razorback it was called. He must have weighed about five hundred pounds. I was glad I never came upon him. Pa said the thing would have torn me up given the chance.

When Wade Farley reached the edge of Crowley's Ridge he pulled up short. Stepping down from his mount he tied the horse off and skedaddled up the side of the ridge on foot. Captain Bowlin held us up where we were, leaving us standing in about two feet of murky water.

A fly buzzed my cheek and Captain Bowlin whispered, "If you smack that fly you're going to get somebody killed."

I held steady while the fly buzzed about me, landed and then buzzed some more. A water moccasin slithered across the top of the water about ten yards up the trail and I suddenly became calm in my saddle. Birds were chirping on either side of us in the distance, and I wondered what they were saying to one another. It was hot and it was muggy, but we stood still, not making a sound.

In a few minutes Wade came back down the ridge and waved for the captain. "Hold your position men."

We watched as Captain Bowlin and Wade discussed what the scout had seen. There were animals in the forest,

in this case a liquid forest, which rarely makes contact with humans. Take a cat for instance. A cat will find all sorts of ways not to be seen by the eyes of man. On this particular day, we encountered the one cat in the forest that just didn't care. "Men, slowly remove your hats and cover the eyes of you horse," John Stone said. I did just like John Stone instructed, and there, cutting a trail right between us and the captain was a large bobcat. He looked our way for a moment, and then he looked at the captain. Just in time, Captain Bowlin and Wade got the eyes of their horses covered. The cat strolled by and was soon out of sight.

"All clear," John informed us.

Even I knew what would have happened if our horses had seen that cat. They would have started pitching and fussing like untamed bronco's ready to throw any rider. They would have bolted and there would have been so much noise we would have surely given away our position. I thanked my lucky stars that I was riding with men who had experience in a swamp environment that day. They were good.

Captain Bowlin motioned us forward and John softly added, "Come on men."

When we reached the ridge we all stepped down in order to give our mounts a well-needed break.

"Men, there's at least a dozen Yankee's up there and they appear to be lost. They're setting up camp to stay the night. We're going to ride back and find Sheriff Wright and his posse and lead them right to them. Are there any concerns among you?"

"No sir," we all responded in a whisper.

"All right then, we walk our horses out of here. Wade, lead the way."

Everything that had been said in the last half hour was nothing more than a whisper. We took up our reins and followed Wade as he led us around the Yankee encampment. They were pitching their tents near the old Sawmill Road. Sawmill Road was pretty much Main Street from Missouri down to Gainesville and Parmalay. They were likely to meet all kinds of travelers if they were encamped on that road. Most likely they were off the road a ways.

When we were almost a mile away from their position the captain instructed us to mount up. We walked our horses for another mile or so and then we set them to a gallop. Keep in mind we were traveling a narrow road through the forest on top of Crowley's Ridge. Chances are we wouldn't see anyone for an hour or two, but you never knew who might be out traveling on a night such as this. We could just as well run into another Yankee detachment lost in the woods.

An hour later just about dusk as we were giving our horses a blow we heard someone coming. Then we heard the voice of Sheriff Wright and we all knew what to do. As we mounted up Captain Bowlin yelled down the lane at the oncoming men, his voice unmistakable, "Sheriff Wright you son-of-a..."

We never heard the rest to of the statement because Bowlin's gun was doing his talking for him, but the hook was set. There was no doubt in Sheriff Wright's mind who he had encountered. After about a minute of deliberate gunfire Captain Bowlin yelled again, "Come on men, let's ride!"

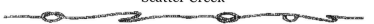

We took off and while the sun had set we could tell that the sheriff and his posse were on our heels about two hundred yards back. We didn't run our horses to death, but we didn't trot them either. The sheriff meant business and it wasn't exactly dark yet.

It only took us about thirty minutes to get back to those Yankee's and we peeled off the road to go around their camp. It had become fairly dark as we did so and we could tell that the company of men had been alerted with the occasional gunfire and the sound of running horses. They were all up to watch us as we rode by their position.

When we circled around to the other side we pulled up and hailed the camp, "Don't shoot, we're friendly," John Stone yelled. This was only possible because none of us wore a uniform.

"What's going on," one of them yelled back.

"We ran into a nest of rebels down the road, they're coming straight for us."

No sooner had John finished his statement they were on us. The Yankee's began to fire at will and so did Sheriff Wright and his men, but rather than sit around and watch the festivities, Captain Bowlin gave his orders without saying a word. We turned our horses and rode away from the gunfight which was exactly as intended.

We aimed our horses north on old Sawmill Road and I knew where the road led. We weren't but maybe five or seven miles from the Pfeiffer place. Gunfire was consistent in the evening air over my shoulder, but we rode calm as if nothing were going on, at least the men around me did. I was a little expectant of a stray bullet which made me all kinds of nervous.

Not until we were over the next ridge did I relax a little knowing that a bullet, no matter how terrible, couldn't cut through that much earth. I wondered what the men I rode with were thinking. As a young man with little war experience, I was having all manner of calamities running through my own mind, but thank God they were only in my mind or I should have never survived the next few days.

The Grim Reaper was circling Duke John Robinson with a sickle in each hand and he was just swinging away, at least in my mind. I jumped at the slightest sound which came from any direction I wasn't looking. Recognizing my plight Captain Bowlin gave me what for.

"Settle down, Duke. You're beginning to make me nervous."

It was the dark of night. As we rode a bobcat screeched in the forest nearby and I almost jumped out of my skin. The thing I was certain of right at that moment was: a body's soul could be scared out of him! I was feeling it, although I hadn't quite left my body, I was certain that once separated, you couldn't get back to where you once belonged, which led to even more worry on my part. What was it that caused a man's soul to separate itself from the physical element of the human body? What would it take for a soul to be so scared that it could leap from the human skeleton? As I asked the question of myself I also realized I didn't want to know the answer to such a question, because in my book there was only one way to find out.

I knew there were folks who didn't believe in God, who didn't believe that a person even had a soul, but I can tell you they're wrong, dead wrong! I considered such

people the walking dead—folks who were ignorant of God's plan. God makes his presence known to those who believe in him, but to those who don't, I say this, God does not correct them, because they are not his children. Lately I was beginning to wonder if I hadn't strayed completely. Was I still a child of God? I hadn't seen much evidence of late which indicated I was anywhere near God, but I couldn't have been more wrong. The men I rode with were God fearing men, and not criminals as Sheriff Wright would have everyone believe.

I wanted to get even with the Starr family, the only justification I felt of late had been shooting Bubba, but I was not satisfied with only that. I seemed to be riding everywhere but the Starr family holdings. Had Joker headed home? I wanted that dog, but the way I was riding of late had me nowhere near him. My hope was that the Wagoner's would feed the wolf hound regular and keep him away from the Star family.

I began to take stock as we rode. What was I doing? I was learning a great deal from these men, but was this type of education something I needed to know? I certainly didn't like being around gunfire. Suddenly I realized that the guns behind me had fallen silent. Who had won? The Yankee's or Sheriff Wright and his men? Right then I humbled myself, realizing many men had probably died because of us. While we had not forced a fight between them, we had set the battle up.

Captain Nathaniel Bowlin was ahead of me as our rogue outfit continued its navigation to the Pfeiffer farm. With a sudden feeling that my outfit was special, I began to understand why the captain was referred to as the Swamp Fox. He had just placed two enemies in battle

against one another, and rode away without a care in the world. He had done so on purpose. Not one of us had fired a shot. It didn't matter to the commander who won the skirmish, Captain Bowlin and his men would be better off.

As we picked our way through the forest on Crowley's Ridge I took note of several facts. What's going to happen is going to happen, the future comes for you bright and early every morning whether a boy is ready for it or not. I had recently seen how the world was treating people, so I began to wonder if I wouldn't be better off to have the Lord as my best friend, and lastly, I had a unique understanding of dumb luck. Dumb luck is God putting together the pieces of the puzzle that you can't see on your own. I'd take that any day.

We had not left the dark ages; we had but put a modern face on them. The weapons we used were the latest advancements in guns, and manufacturers such as Winchester and Smith & Wesson were learning how to mass produce their products for both sides. This was sobering to me.

Pa had always said, "Never fight your battles alone. Always keep God in your corner. He's the best trainer anyway." I always wondered what he meant by that, but while in St. Louis I had seen a few boxing matches and learned that each boxer had a trainer in the corner. After watching how the trainers took care of their fighters, Pa's statement was no longer a mystery to me. Suddenly I thought, a young man shouldn't go out looking for trouble, life will provide for him all the trouble he can handle.

A tree branch I hadn't seen swiped my hat off my head and I stopped to pick it up. I was bringing up the rear and suddenly I realized I had been falling behind while distracted by my own thoughts. Stepping back into the saddle I quickly closed up the gap and paid more attention. The night was quiet, only the occasional squeaking from a leather saddle as we rode along the ridge. Suddenly I wondered, how do you stop a leather saddle from squeaking? It was going to get me killed one of these days. For now we were riding in friendly territory, but I knew that wouldn't always be the case. What could I possibly use to quiet my saddle? I began to run various things through my mind, and the only thing I could come up with seemed to be lye soap. If the Pfeiffer's had some, I knew what I was going to be doing come morning.

Chapter 14

The following morning I got my hands on some lye soap and I began to scrub my saddle with it. I was rubbing my saddle down good when I noticed a small group of men coming through the front gate near the bottom of the hill. Their leader seemed to be a tall slim man in a white suit wearing a white hat. As they drew near I could see he had a peacock feather sticking out from the left side. When they stopped at the front porch I saw the silver stars on his collar. I was looking at my first general.

"General Thompson, good to see you," Mr. Pfeiffer said as he came out onto the front porch, Captain Bowlin following close behind. "General, I would like you to meet Captain Nathanial Bowlin, the Swamp Fox," he said as he took hold of the front porch railing.

"Well now, I also am known as the Swamp Fox, but I am unfamiliar with the captain's uniform," General Thompson stated.

"Sir," Bowlin saluted, "We wish to appear as civilians, nothing more. Should we wear the Confederate uniform we would be easy pickings for the Yankee's just to our north."

Thompson perked up. "Yanks? Do you suggest there are Federal troops in the area?"

"Yes sir. We ran into a small cluster just last night about seven miles south of here on the Gainesville-Helena road."

"I take it you dispatched them."

"No sir, we let Sheriff Wright and his men shoot it out with them. Once we had a fair skirmish started my men and I rode away."

"And the sheriff didn't object?"

"Sir, the sheriff killed my brother and my brother-in-law recently. Reports are that he had Jesse shot in the head while he lay wounded on the ground. No matter which side won last night, I feel my men were on the winning side."

"I see. Hence the title Swamp Fox."

"Yes sir," Bowlin acknowledged.

"Pfeiffer, I hear through the grapevine that the Yankee's have placed a price on my head. Do you know anything about it?"

Mr. Pfeiffer didn't answer right away. Instead, he said, "General, won't you come inside and have a cool glass of tea?"

"That would be splendid. Ajax," he said as he turned to his big Indian friend, "Take Sardanapalus and get him some oats. Take care of Goat Weed too." He stepped down from his saddle and handed the reins to the Indian. As he turned his back to me I noticed the general carried a long ivory handled knife behind his back, slipped through his belt. I didn't know it then, but the general never went anywhere without that knife.

There were two other men with the general who had stopped near the water trough down by the barn to water their horses as the men came into the yard. They were meandering about talking about something in a low tone, I couldn't hear. I probably wouldn't know what they were talking about anyway, but a boy does like to learn, especially in times like these.

I continued to rub soap into the saddle leather and soon I had anywhere one piece of leather might rub against another covered. The saddle wasn't squeaking near as much it seemed, but I wouldn't be sure until I actually had it mounted on my horse. The hard part was trying to work the soap up into the tight places where I couldn't even get a finger in.

Once I finished I wrapped up my soap bar and placed the remainder in my saddle bag. The soap had been given me by Mrs. Pfeiffer earlier that morning. She had an entire basketful which she was adept at making. She had special soaps which contained lavender, cinnamon, rose pedals and sage. Her favorite, she told me, was the lavender, and I must agree the lavender had the best aroma of all. Mrs. Barbara Pfeiffer was proud of her soaps as she was her children.

There were four children at home, four which actually belonged to Mrs. Pfeiffer and three others who had been loosely adopted. All of them were gently ushered out of the house while the two Swamp Fox's met inside. What they were discussing I had no idea, but I was wishful to be getting my own horse under me. How exactly I was going to do such a thing was the question. I was thirty-five or forty miles away from home. My gut was telling me I need not let the situation fester too long, but the war and every man around me seemed to have a different motive for the moment.

As we had special guests about, when lunch was served Mrs. Pfeiffer dug out a jar of Mr. Pfeiffer's special pickled catfish. I had no idea that catfish could taste that good. Hesitant as I was to taste it I only got a little piece

like everyone else, but I could have eaten the entire jar on my own. Pickled catfish is a delicacy in Northeast Arkansas.

To make a long story short, when I learned that General Thompson was headed to Pocahontas, I asked permission to side him in order to stop at the Starr farm and retrieve my horse, saddle, and other belongings, as well as my sister, I hoped. After explaining the matter more thoroughly, General Thompson would have it no other way, so later that afternoon as he and his men saddled up I joined them and we headed into the swamp. I was also going along as a guide because I had grown up in the area and I knew my way to and fro.

General Thompson was a strict disciplinarian. He was tall, lanky, and possessed a long sharp nosed face with blue eyes and yellow hair. The hair he combed back behind his ears where it flowed down below his collar. I learned that his real name was Meriwether by the time we made it to Peach Orchard. Here we stopped for the evening and I knew the next day was going to tell all. In my estimation, Nathaniel Bowlin was the Swamp Fox here about Greene County, but this general insisted he was *the* Swamp Fox.

The next morning when we rode out from Peach Orchard after a good breakfast with the Wagoner's who'd insisted we stay the night, I got my understanding of why the general was also considered a fox. As we were headed for the Starr ranch, I led us by the old homestead then into the swamp to the west. On horseback it didn't take us long to reach the Starr place.

When we rode into the yard, I had Mike riding double behind me. This was so he could take Ol' Sho-me home with him once I had Jericho back in my possession.

Franklyn Starr met us on the front porch and I could tell that he was more nervous than usual. In times past he would have come out yelling for us to get off his property, but not this morning. Something was different. What I had no idea.

"Mr. Starr, I believe you have a horse, saddle and rigging in your possession which belongs to this young man. Will you hand them over peacefully or shall we take them?"

"Well, first of all, I don't know you from…" Starr began.

"The name is General Thompson. Now, will you hand over the young man's belongings, or do we take them?"

"Well sir, I…"

"Ajax, take the boy and get his horse."

Starr began to protest and I saw the general slide his revolver from under his white coat. It was pointed directly at Starr before I even knew he had one.

"I know when I am dealing with a sneaking coward, Captain Starr. You're one of those cowardly dogs who have never done a stinking thing on either side, yet you call yourself a captain. I hope beyond all hope that the Federals find their way this far south and hang you for the heartless dog you are, wherever they find you."

We could hear him all the way over to the corral. Ajax put a lead halter and rope on Jericho and into the barn we went. That Indian didn't miss a thing. He was expecting trouble, and when it came he was ready for it. He shoved me out of the way and with one motion, lifted his tomahawk and buried it into the chest of a man I didn't know. He had been laying for us just inside the barn door. His pistol, which was pointed at me, went off into the

ground directly at my feet, scaring the wits out of me. Had I been two feet closer he would have nailed me. The man fell backward and his gun slipped from his hand as he clutched at the weapon impaled in his chest. He squirmed for a moment and then just as he pulled the tomahawk out, he took his last breath. I looked back to see what was happening at the front porch. The general was still in control.

I didn't need any orders, I found my saddle, bridle and blanket, put them up on Jericho as fast as I could. I know he had been lame, but that was weeks ago and if no one had ridden him it was a good bet he had healed up by now.

While Ajax was cinching everything tight I walked back to the tack room and retrieved my saddle bag and rifle. Placing the saddlebags on my horse I slipped the rifle into the scabbard and tied the saddle bag down. Then I stepped into the saddle and rode out of the barn with Ajax walking behind me.

I rode him to the front of the house where the general and his men sat waiting. Just then my little sister and little brother came walking out onto the porch with Mrs. Starr. I swallowed hard. Suddenly, I knew what it was to have my heart ripped from my chest. The man that had killed my Pa was raising my brother and sister. I was speechless. I didn't have a clue what to say. My mouth tried to form words which would not come.

"Is that all of your gear, Duke?"

All I could do was shake my head up and down at the general. Like I said, I was speechless.

"All right then, Starr, if you try anything while we're riding away, I'll personally hang you myself," the general threatened.

Turning his horse the general led us out of the yard back into the swamp. I looked back over my shoulder longingly wanting to talk to my brother and sister, but I could do nothing. I had known about my little sister, but they had my brother too! Why had they brought them out onto the porch? To make sure I knew he had them? Why? Deep down I knew why. If anything else happened to the Starr family which was my doing, my own brother and sister would be their next victims.

I tried to think of anything good which might change my answer, but nothing came to me. It was plain as day. If I didn't leave the Starr family alone, my brother and sister would pay. Did they know? Of course not, they were already victims, too young to know what men were capable of. What were they being told? I could bet money it wasn't the truth.

"General Thompson, sir," I said as we rode. "The boy and girl on the front porch are my brother and sister. I can't leave them in the hands of the Starr family."

"I knew there was more going on here than meets the eye. Where we're headed is no place for the likes of children that age. We'll have to pick them up on the way back."

"They are in real danger, sir."

"It can't be helped, son. That's the best I can do."

It seemed to me that the Starr holdings were only good as long as they could steal from others without being caught. At least that's what it looked like to me. How could I, Duke John Robinson at the age of fifteen do

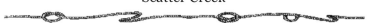

anything which would uncover their diabolical ways? How could I save my little brother and sister from certain ruination at the hands of the Starr family? The answer seemed impossible. Nothing in my mind would allow me to believe that I could do anything to change the course of events where my fellow siblings were concerned unless I could get them away from Captain Starr.

My thoughts were occasionally interrupted by the fact I had to give directions as to which way to turn in the swamp between the Starr ranch and Pocahontas which was a town that sat up on the ridge overlooking the Black River. We would have to ford the river once we got close to town, but I knew the crossing well. There was a sharp turn to the south and if we entered the river just ahead of the turn the current was such that it would carry us to the other side easily. Coming back was a different crossing.

As we drew near the crossing the general quizzed me.

"Duke, are you sure there's no other way to get across?"

"Not unless they've built a bridge in the last few years. I haven't been here for that long, but my guess is, nothing has changed. The war has seen to that," I added.

As we neared the crossing the general saw something to our south and pulled up. "What does that look like to you, Duke?"

"Looks like a bridge sir," I said sheepishly.

"Man is always building something, son. Remember that."

Turning our horses we headed for the new river crossing. The old ones worked fine, but you had to get wet. Some horses didn't like getting wet and would pitch a fit. Others didn't mind at all.

As we lumbered our horses across the wooden structure, the hollow sound spooked them. At first they didn't want to go, but they settled down finally and followed their commands. Ajax had the least amount of trouble with his horse and I wondered just what that Indian knew. One thing was certain he sure seemed comfortable in the white man's world.

General Thompson kept looking at the bridge and suddenly he said, "I know this type of construction. This is Yankee doings. Duke, do you know of any Yankee's this far south?"

"Sir, I haven't heard of any except over on the Mississippi, but I haven't exactly been home much these last two years. They could be right here."

"This is a Yankee footbridge. Stay alert men. We might be walking into a Yankee encampment." With Thompson's warning every single one of us were suddenly thrust into another norm, one which had us on edge. We had no reason to doubt the general's deduction. If he thought there were Yankee's about, then there probably were. All his men suddenly pulled their pistols and checked them to be sure they were fully loaded, so I didn't hesitate to do the same.

The first horses we encountered were tied to the hitch rail on the town square, and they all wore a U S brand. We pulled back into the alleyway and the general looked my way.

"Duke, is there a back way to the hotel on the other side of the square?"

"Yes sir, but it sure is a long way around."

"Then lead the way. I'm not ready to hand myself over to the Yankee's just yet," he stated.

I eased my horse back down the ridge toward the river and took to the riverbank. We stayed out of the water, but below the tree line as much as possible in order to keep out of sight of prying eyes. Once the river turned east I kept riding north until I found the meadow I was looking for, then I turned west along the tree line to circle the town under cover. It had been my hope that the Yankee's didn't have a unit of regulars encamped at the meadow, as it was close to town, but my luck was with me and no one was there.

As we rode up into the hills from there I kept a sharp eye out. The last thing I wanted to do was be responsible for getting General Thompson caught and made into a prisoner of war. The hills were steep at this point, but there was nothing I could do about it. I had to ride the point and be aware. What I couldn't believe was the fact these grown men trusted me to lead them in.

I couldn't help but notice that the only saddle not squeaking had been Michaels, and he was no longer with us. I didn't say a word, but did become certain of one thing. The moment I got a chance I was going to lather up my own saddle with Mrs. Pfeiffer's soap. It was squeaking something awful.

As we neared town General Thompson ordered a halt. "We'll wait here until dark. Once we have the cover of darkness we'll sneak into the hotel."

We made our camp in the woods and Ajax disappeared. I didn't pretend to know what for, but if he was going into town, he was going to stick out like a sore thumb.

What I didn't realize was, Indian's had immunity where the war was concerned. It was a white man's war,

not an Indian war. He could go anywhere he wanted, north or south and no one the wiser.

When he returned he had information which the general needed. "Only one room left, so I bought it. Hotel full of Yankee's, but I can sneak you up the back stairs."

"Good, I could use a good night's rest in a good bed. This sleeping out under the stars is getting to my lower back."

We settled in then and broke out some bread rolls Mrs. Wagoner had given us at Peach Orchard, added a few slices of deer meat to spice it up and made certain we didn't go hungry. We had it cold and we drank water with our meager supper. There was to be no fire this close to town. The Indian and General Thompson had gone to the hotel, leaving the rest of us to suffer the night air.

Being only a young man I thought I might also have immunity enough to walk around the square, so I too headed for town with a warning ringing in my ears.

"Be careful, Duke."

That was Harold Webster doing the talking, he and William Boudreau of the 3rd Louisiana were the two men assigned to shadow the general and keep him safe. I took heed and made my way to the town square. Taking a seat on the park bench near the courthouse, I settled into watching what the Yanks were up to. It didn't take long for me to duck and run. Captain Starr and his foreman rode into the square almost immediately. They hadn't seen me, but if I hung around they were going to.

I ducked behind some bushes and to my amazement the Captain Starr rode right up to the hotel. He spoke to some Yankee's who were lounging on the front porch rail smoking and momentarily they dowsed their cigarettes

and all went inside. In a few minutes I could hear some commotion and they drug the general out of the St. Charles hotel in handcuffs. Starr was beaming with a smile from ear to ear.

"There you go gentlemen, now where do I collect my reward?"

"First we'll have to verify a few things, but you'll get your reward if this fellow is who you say he is," one of the Yanks responded.

"What will we do with this Indian, Captain Gentry?"

"Turn him loose, he's not wanted."

"Hold on, captain. He killed one of my men earlier today while he was in my barn. I would like a chance to settle up with him," Starr smiled.

"Starr, it shall be my pleasure to see you hang," Thompson snarled.

"Unfortunately, you're going to hang first."

"Turn me loose and let me at him," Thompson cried. "This man is the slime of the earth. Just give me five minutes, that's all I ask."

"I almost wish I could, general. Now, if you don't mind we are taking a walk down to the jail." The Yankee captain shoved General Thompson in the direction of the jail and I knew just how low down Captain Starr was. The general was correct in his estimation. Captain Star was a coward, and a cutthroat, a thief that retribution awaited.

Chapter 15

I remained behind the bushes until the street was clear of Yankee troops and then I began to cautiously survey the rest of the square. I slipped out of my hiding spot and looked around the corner of the courthouse. The street was quiet so I took in after Captain Starr and the Indian. Those men had a noose around his neck when they led him away and they were looking for a tree. It was in my mind to make sure they didn't hang Ajax, but I had to be on time.

It didn't take long for me to find them. They were just outside of the town square and already had the rope over a tree limb. As they tied the rope off, I walked into the picture with my pistol drawn.

"Cut him loose, captain!"

"What? You again?" Starr was incredulous.

"You're not hanging anybody tonight, not even an Indian. We've have had about enough of your shenanigans. If you don't cut him down right this minute, I'm going to fill you full of holes and you know what? My conscience will be clear." I shut up then and let my words sink in, worried the entire time that he would somehow make my brother and sister pay for my actions.

It was do or die. I might only be fifteen years old, but I had shot Bubba and taken my gun back, and I had taken the dog. The thing was, a gun doesn't care how old the finger on the trigger is, if the finger twitches, squeezes or pulls, the gun will fire and Starr knew it.

I had him pegged for the coward he was. They cut the Indian loose and I instructed them to get on their horses and ride.

"If we see you on the morrow it will be a gunfight. I won't wait on you to draw, I'll just shoot on sight," I said. Well, Van Cleve and Starr rode out with their tails tucked. They didn't want to die, they just wanted to collect their reward, but that reward was going to have to wait.

"Thanks," Ajax said. "They would have hung me."

"Just return the favor sometime. I may need it, or someone else."

"Let's get back to horses. We have to get out of town," Ajax replied.

We didn't talk anymore, we just skirted the town to stay out of harm's way and eventually we made it back to camp. Webster and Boudreau were waiting on us.

"We didn't expect to see you," Boudreau said to Ajax.

"The Yankee's have captured the general."

The men who had been lounging against their saddles sat bolt upright, "Can we get him back?" Boudreau wanted to know.

"Maybe, but we need patience."

"This isn't going to look good on our resume," Webster commented.

"You're not just whistling Dixie. If we don't get the general back we'll never get promoted."

"Let's saddle up and get out of here before the Yankee's figure out the general isn't traveling alone," I advised.

The last thing I wanted was to get caught holding the general's horse and saddle for him. There was a time to play and a time to run, and right now was a time to run.

We saddled up our mounts and I led us out of there to the north, looking for an old trail which would take us around any Yankee's and the Starr family. With news of the general in town, the bridge would now be watched.

General Thompson sat with his hands tied to a chair. He was purposefully trying to make himself comfortable as possible when his counterpart walked into the room.

"Well, I'll be a monkey's uncle. Joseph Hooker! Of all the people to bump into in Arkansas," the general said.

"Meriwether Jeff Thompson. It has been a long time since West Point."

"A lot of water under the bridge, my old friend."

"I was expecting anyone but an old classmate."

"I could say the same."

"You know, you're fighting for the wrong side."

"Oh, how so?"

The room was dark and dry, but the small oil lamp lit all four walls rather well. A small table holding the lamp sat against the east wall and the chair to which Meriwether found himself tied completed the furniture in the small jail cell. Not even a cot had found its way into the unusually small chamber. A quirt was hanging on the wall near the table.

"The south has a problem which it can do nothing about," Hooker stated.

"And what would that be?" Meriwether asked.

"Modern warfare demands centralized leadership for any measurable productivity and the subordination of everything toward the war effort. This is a fact which stands at odds with President Jackson's misguided adherence to State's Rights my friend."

"Well, at least the south doesn't have to pass laws forcing their men to join the fight against their will," Thompson challenged.

"You mean the Enrollment Act of March 3rd?"

"Exactly. You're still trying to quell the riots in New York City, you now have a war on two fronts."

"We'll handle it," Hooker said.

"While you're doing that, Lee will be carving up Washington."

"I can see there's no convincing you otherwise, so I'll be shipping you to St. Louis in the morning."

"I suppose I should thank you."

"You could thank me by swearing allegiance to the Federal Government," Hooker offered.

"I'd rather sit in jail."

"Still the same Ol' Thompson." After a slight pause, "Guard?"

I found the trail about three miles north of town so we crossed Hamil Creek and made our way back into the swamp via an old slough north of the Black River called Throgmorton. I led the men through the shallow water of the slough to cover our horse tracks and headed west. Ajax had the general's horse in tow. Webster and Boudreau were behind me while Ajax brought up the rear.

How do I describe the country we were riding in, trees were everywhere, it was a swamp most of the year and it was now. The horses were stepping in mush, over fallen tree branches, and downed logs. The undergrowth was thick this time of year. There was no way to make time in such an environment. When we found a hammock which was high and dry we made a dry camp for the night.

We picketed the horses and unsaddled them. Then we dug out our blanket rolls and settled in. I was certain we had extinguished any sign of tracks by navigating Throgmorton Slough so when I closed my eyes that evening I was pleased with myself. About two hours later, near midnight, we heard thunder rumbling in the distance and all of us got up. We broke camp, saddled our mounts and stepped into leather.

In ten minutes we were soaking wet. We each had a poncho which helped, but not much. My hat was soaked through and water was running down the side of my head and neck into my clothes. In no time at all I was getting wet down under. It was going to be a long night!

When it's dry, you can navigate a swamp pretty good. When it's wet you can forget it. All I wanted was to find our next stop, and the only thing I could think of was the Murphy farm. I didn't even know if I could find the place in such a downpour, but as the sun began to light the morning to a dull gray I saw the barn roof in the distance. Shelter!

"There's what we're looking for," I said over my shoulder pointing a finger in the direction of the structure. The barn was unpainted when most folks wanted a red one with white trim. Given time I was certain that Murphy's barn would also turn a dignified shade of red.

We made our way around the rain soaked field to the barn door. I jumped down and opened it up wide so we could get our horses in out of the rain. They all filed in one by one then I led Jericho in last and closed the door behind me. Murphy's house was a quarter mile away across the field to our west. In this rain there was ought to worry about.

We all began to shed our wet clothes right down to our dungarees, hanging them anywhere we could to let them dry. What we needed was a good warm fire, but that wasn't going to happen, not with a barn full of hay.

Uncomfortable, miserable and cold, that was how we were getting along. Our horses on the other hand were in horse heaven, out of the rain, munching hay and resting comfortable. The disparity was sobering for I had to dress, mount my horse and ride to Murphy's house and let him know what we were up to so that he didn't go off like a loaded gun. I knew old man Murphy had a temper, especially when he was set upon by strangers. What we were doing wasn't much different, setting up on his property without his knowledge or permission, but he was a reasonable fellow when informed.

I finally struggled into my damp clothes knowing I had a job to do and saddled up Jericho. The men waved as I rode out into the rain soaked field and headed for the house.

I reached the Murphy home in a relatively short time, yet no one seemed to be there. I looked inside the small barn beside the house and the carriage and horse were both gone. Cursing my luck I turned Jericho back for the Murphy barn where my friends were waiting. I had gotten wet for no reason, but I had no way of knowing. I would have to try again. My guess was he'd return once the rain let up. Nobody liked driving a wagon or a carriage in the rain, least of all Mr. Murphy.

Everyone but Ajax was sleeping when I returned to the barn. Ol' Ajax was a very slippery sort of character. If I paid attention, I might learn a lot from the Indian. He didn't talk much, but when he did it was to the point.

"Deliver message?"

"No one was home," I explained.

"Bad sign," Ajax warned. "I go."

"You might as well stay," I said. "Murphy won't be back for a while, so no harm. When he does return, I'll see to it he knows we're here."

"You trust too much."

"I trust because I know Mr. Murphy. He's a good man we can count on. He rides with Nathanial Bowlin often," I stated.

"In that case, Ajax stay," the Indian agreed.

We made ourselves as comfortable as possible while the rain continued to pour outside. An occasional clap of lightning or thunder rolled through the eaves of the barn as I got out of my wet clothes once again and settled in to get warm. Something about being cold and wet did not set well with me. The spot I found was in the corner behind the door and I pushed some hay up into a good bed and lay down. All I had on was my undergarment, but even it was wet. I knew in time it would dry out, but my other clothes would dry best hanging on the nail by the door. I even hung my socks up to dry though what they really needed was a good washing.

There was nothing any of us could do to save General Thompson. Whatever the Yankee's planned to do with him they would do. We would get little chance to set him free. Being a general captured in the field, he would be shipped to a prison somewhere. The men I now rode with intended to stop it, but I had no idea how. All I could envision was bloodshed.

My mission as I saw it was to report the capture to Captain Bowlin as soon as the rain let up long enough to

ride. I had no way of knowing good weather would take three days. Three days of nonstop rain filled our schedule and kept us from an uncertain destiny. This was a time of learning for me, a time to listen to the men in the group. And I hung on every word. It was my intention to live through this ugly war, and I would need to garner all of the knowledge I could in order to do so.

In the first light of morning the first day in Murphy's barn I awoke to find a fresh meal prepared by the hands of Mrs. Murphy. Seems Mr. Murphy had been to the barn later the previous day and found us there. He recognized me and said, "Let the boy sleep. I'll have the wife bring you breakfast in the morning."

The others were sitting around eating at my expense. If I had not awaken when I did the food would have been gone with me none the wiser. I looked at those men when I saw what was left for me and I knew I didn't have to say a word in order to convict them. I picked up the tray which held the meager remains of breakfast and made my way back to my bed. As I finished off the scant remains of food my eyes studied the mongrels which would have let me starve, for the day anyhow. I didn't have to say a word as my eyes held all of the conviction necessary.

"I suppose ya'll think it funny," I accused setting the dish aside.

"It would have been, but you woke up and spoiled our play," Boudreau admitted.

"I'll have to be on my toes around you fellows if I plan to eat."

"You can count on it," Webster said with a mischievous grin.

I was not sure whether to thank them or hit them, but I kept my cool and settled into my corner for some more rest. The rain was pouring down outside so we weren't going anywhere at all.

"General Thomson is probably more comfortable than us right this minute," Boudreau suggested.

"He might be, but we have got to come up with a plan to get him back," added Webster.

I listened with care. I might not know as much as these men, but around here I knew more than most.

"In this rain we won't be crossing the river unless we cross that Yankee built bridge."

"They won't have any guards posted in this weather," Webster offered.

"Don't you bet on it. Them Yankee's are liable to have the whole army keeping an eye on that bridge."

Talk is what men do when there is nothing else to do, and with such weather as we had outside the barn, there was nothing to do but let them talk. I did plenty of listening. I did some thinking too.

I didn't want this war, but it was on me whether I wanted it or not. There was no way for me to avoid the conflict now. I was in the war up to my neck and all this boy wanted was to go west. The fact the Starr family had two of my siblings bothered me some. How had they ended up with the likes of Bubba and his brothers? We had never gotten along with the Starr's, and here they were living in the same home. I just couldn't understand how such a thing could happen. I still had three other sisters somewhere.

The last thing I remembered, my brother and sisters had been left in the hands of the Pruitt family over near

Parmalay. How had they gotten all the way back home? The Starr ranch wasn't home, but it was right next door to where our home had stood, and where were my other siblings?

Anywhere is a God awful place to be an orphan, but to be living in the Starr home, I just couldn't imagine. What had happened to cause them to be there? It was the one thing which just didn't make a bit of sense to me. No way or no how could I figure that my brother and sister got to the Starr household, but they were there just as pretty as you please.

The war! This war was causing all kinds of grief for families, not just mine. How simple of me to be thinking selfishly. I was not the only person who had lost family of late. Look at Michael, and I had five brothers and sisters who were now orphans.

Who would be left when the war was over? There was little doubt more men, women, and children would die. How long does a war last? I couldn't understand much more than that at the moment, which meant I had no idea how a war could evolve. My thoughts on the matter were one dimensional. Suddenly I knew my inability to think in larger terms was a handicap born of my youth, a pure disadvantage when dealing with grown men. Such a stumbling block would have to be removed if I were to survive the war. Why? Because I was right smack dab in the middle of it. There was nowhere for Duke John Robinson to hide.

When the storm finally relented, the land was pure mud outside. After three days of being cooped up in a barn with the other fellows I was ready to ride, only they were heading back to Pocahontas to see if they could free

the general. I was going home. I had to reach the Pfeiffer place to get word to Captain Bowlin about the capture. The one thing on my mind which might stop me was Franklyn Starr. If I ran into him it would be a shootout. I had promised him one and there would be no one to help me.

The Murphy's had been more than kind by feeding us all three days. I waved goodbye as I rode past the house. Murphy knew what was up. He had visited us in the barn and he knew our plans. We were on our own now. He had done all he could for us. Ajax and the soldiers were on their way back to Pocahontas to free the general.

The last thing we had done before leaving the barn was to muck out the stalls where the horses had stayed. Mr. Murphy had requested we do so, and it was a foregone conclusion we would have done it anyway as leaving a mess at your neighbor's house is impolite.

Jericho sloshed through the forest and made his way to the Wagoner's home at Peach Orchard. There I had lunch then continued on with Michael riding beside me. We had to reach the Pfeiffer farm by nightfall which we did just as the sun was going down.

Captain Bowlin was not there, but Heinrich Pfeiffer was there, and that was all I needed to know. He would tell Captain Bowlin the first chance he got. As for me I was not sure what to do, but Mr. Pfeiffer suggested I stay with them until Bowlin came back through. Michael mounted up to return to the Wagoner's. I told him to be careful and keep an eye out for Captain Starr. My hunch was that Starr would be in Pocahontas until he obtained his reward for his assistance in capturing the general, but a body just never knew for sure one way or the other.

Chapter 16

Captain Bowlin took the news rather well considering he had just lost three men on his raid over into Missouri. He had struck the Yankee's near Charleston only a few miles from the Mississippi. That was about seventy miles give or take and they had ridden hard to reach the Arkansas forest land, what we call the Liquid Forest—swamp land in any other language.

"It's up to Webster and Boudreau to recover the general. We have our hands full here. He's probably already half way to St. Louis by now anyway. They have prisons enough for soldiers up there," Bowlin offered.

"That was a fine thing you did saving that Indian," Pfeiffer said.

"I couldn't let Starr hang another man, not even an Indian."

I looked over at Captain Bowlin, then looked at myself in the dining room mirror and cringed. My face was black and blue, yet no one had said a word. It was from the fight I'd had with Nikoli days before. He had given me a pounding before the men had pulled him off of me. Suddenly I was embarrassed and didn't want to be seen by anyone.

I got up from the table and made my way out to the barn. I looked inside and then walked back to the house. I wasn't about to lie down in that barn. I stretched out on the front porch over in the corner and lay my head back.

Closing my eyes I tried to imagine my world without war, but I could not.

Everyone fairly left me alone at that point, so I managed quite a fair nap in the afternoon shade. Folks would come out onto the porch now and again, but they were coming and going from inside the house. Paying them no mind there was ought to do but rest. The day wore on lazily and before I knew it the bell rang for suppertime. Now a bell was used in those days because it could be heard from a long way off, and some of the men were a good ways from the house when Barbara Pfeiffer rang out her song.

In twenty minutes everyone was at the long table the Pfeiffer's kept for guests and the children were at another. I was still classified as a child so I was not able to sit at the adult table. Had there not been so much company, I could have. One thing I couldn't help but notice was the fact the folks around here liked their chicken and dumplings. Not that I'm complaining, because I surely ain't, but a man does like beef once in a while or even a carved up ham.

I knew where I was going to sleep that evening, and so did Mrs. Pfeiffer. I was going to lay my head to rest on the front porch swing. The men could have the barn. I was a little gun shy after sharing my space with a puff adder my first night on the farm. At sundown Mrs. Pfeiffer brought me a quilt and a pillow and told me if it started raining to come in the house. She was a nice lady, Mrs. Pfeiffer. In the back of my mind I pictured my own mother having been such a woman.

We swamp rats hung around for about three days until Zach Holmes began to show sign of recovery and then we rode out. We rode down the old Sawmill Road a

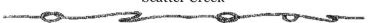

ways until we came upon that Yankee command. The sheriff hadn't even turned a shovel. The Yankee blue were laying all around and the stench was something awful. One thing was obvious from my estimation; Nathaniel Bowlin still had a sheriff to kill.

We spent the day putting them in the ground, and some of them had already been visited by wild animals looking for an easy meal. We saved what few items were left behind and then headed south. About sundown we were ten miles north of Gainesville and Captain Bowlin rode into the yard of Jesse's home. The place had been ransacked, everything taken which wasn't nailed down, and the first order he gave was to put everything back in place, fix the corral post which had been pulled down and feed the horses.

As we built a fire in the fireplace and cooked over an open flame, Captain Bowlin began to shape things up for us in our minds.

"Gentlemen, from this day forward we shall be a thorn in the side of Sheriff Wright. I will still conduct matters of war, but from now on this location will be our outpost. We will not leave it unguarded, ever."

"That sounds good to me," John Stone added. "I been wondering how long you were going to let the sheriff dictate the situation."

"John, if you weren't my friend, I'd shoot you for that!"

"And rightly so," John admitted.

"Nat, why don't I ride into town and see what's bothering that old mossy horn," Bob Eubanks offered. "Besides, I'd like to make sure we took care of the court house."

"Be careful, and get back here just as fast as you can."

Bob Eubanks didn't have to be told what to do. He saddled up his horse to ride out and make inquiries. Bob Eubanks lived over near the Black River and he was the least suspicious when it came to talking to folks in Gainesville. That's what folks did when they came to town, they asked questions and looked to see who was doing what, and that made his mission all the more normal. A man can learn a lot talking to the town folks and listening to their answers.

At the corral fence I leaned up against the top rail and asked, "Bob, would you check on my brother and sisters to see what might have become of them? If it isn't too dangerous," I added.

"I'll see what I can find out," he said as he stepped into the saddle. I opened the gate for him and closed it behind him as he rode away. Turning I walked back to the front porch of the house and sat down on the steps. I had a desire to take care of Franklyn Starr once and for all, but before I did so I wanted to know what he was to my brother and sister. I wanted to know how they got there and I wanted to know if I could get them away.

Suddenly I took a long look around the yard to make certain the grim reaper wasn't out there swinging a wide swath fixing to take me in without my knowledge. That's how it happens you know. Not one person who dies expects to die on that particular day, but something happens, usually in the way of trouble and suddenly a person finds themselves dangling on a hook gasping for precious air, like a fish freshly pulled from the water. Life can be over that quickly, but if the grim reaper was watching me, he was good at keeping himself hidden.

I got up and made my way to the rocking chair on the corner of the front porch, one of the few items Wright and his men hadn't stolen. I sat down in it and closed my eyes, wanting nothing more than to be somewhere else. War will do that to you. I wanted to go to the Rocky Mountains, and here I was bogged down in the middle of somebody else's war. A war I wanted nothing to do with. However, my gut was telling me I was far from finished when it came to Greene County Arkansas and the folks who lived here.

Something had to be done about Sheriff Wright and something had to be done about his friend Captain Franklyn Starr. I knew the rest of the men were in the house making plans for the sheriff of Greene County, but what about Starr? It seemed that I was the only one who had reason to brace him.

I was feeling lonely right then. I can't tell you how lonely I was, but I can tell you, lonely isn't the worst thing that can happen to a child. I had already been tried by the fire if you will, and I didn't like it none, but at that age I didn't understand what trial by fire really was. I didn't know for instance that I could not be a real man until that happened. In my naïve estimation all that was necessary to become a man was to reach a certain age, a birthday if you will. I couldn't have been more wrong.

It takes people doing things to you, mostly things that you aren't going to like, in order to hone and fine tune your skills as a human being, sharpen the blade so to speak. My blade which I'll call my self-esteem, something Captain Bowlin had mentioned once or twice, was being sharpened by the war and in the end would make me a better person, providing I managed to survive. Right then

I didn't know any of that. I thought if I reached twenty one or so I would be a man.

Funny how life works. To the men I rode with I was a man already, but in my mind I didn't recognize this fact. I thought I still had to prove myself to them. Boy, was I ever wrong! You're thinking things are one way when they are really another. I am thankful for my friends, though I didn't know in reality that the men I rode with were my friends. I knew them to a degree, but never did the thought cross my mind that I had friends I could count on.

The sound of horses galloping down the road stirred my attention, and caused me to open my eyes. I opened them to nine horses and riders spreading out in the front yard around me. Fear suddenly took a slow hold of me deep down in my soul, for all I could see in front of me was the grim reaper, and I had just checked for him!

My eyes had settled on Sheriff Wright and his unscrupulous posse, if one could call them a posse at all. They weren't here for any Sunday-go-to-meeting picnic, they had a look of business about them and when the dust settled I was all alone on that front porch with Captain Starr opposite me just staring.

"Well if it ain't Duke John Robinson," he let out in a deep sly southern drawl. "I figured you had done skedaddled by now." He paused and then he said, "Remember what you told me, boy? What you told me the last time you saw me?" He paused for he certainly wanted me to remember what I had said. I remembered real well, I would kill him on sight. It would be a gunfight without hesitation. Only I had not expected to be so outnumbered.

"You said you'd kill me." He paused again, "Well, I'm waiting, boy."

Slowly I got up from my rocking chair and stood erect. I looked at the sheriff and spoke. "He killed my pa, and if you boys don't mind standing aside, I'm going to make amends," I said as I removed the thong from my six gun.

Eight riders backed away from the situation, giving me the freedom to take care of my grievance with Captain Starr, and suddenly he looked around at his friends and his face turned white. "Where are you fella's going?"

"Ain't our fight," Wright said.

"Well captain, are you going to draw or are you going to sit there like a coward?" I challenged.

From inside the house I heard these words. "If anybody else draws a weapon, we'll be obliged to empty some saddles!"

I had the feeling I was facing a simple coward. Suddenly I just didn't give a flip anymore. I dragged my shooting iron and began firing. Captain Starr jumped down behind his horse and pulled his own gun. His first shot from over his saddle missed and busted an oil lamp hanging near the front door. The coward was hiding behind the bulk of his horse.

I immediately realized it might take all five of my shots to get him because he wouldn't stand still. Understanding my plight, I didn't stand still either. I ducked down low and put a bullet at his legs under his horse, another clean miss. His next bullet whizzed by my head and it had been too close for comfort. It dawned on me then I couldn't win a fight trying to dodge his bullets like he was doing mine and I jumped down off the front

porch landing on my feet. Again I shot at his legs. This time I hit something. He stumbled, but didn't fall. With one hand gripping his saddle horn he aimed his pistol and I dove for the ground where I put another bullet in his leg. Still the man would not go down. A bullet kicked up dirt at my face and blinded me for a moment. I scratched at my eyes to get the dirt out of them, and when I looked up the horse was gone from between us and I was looking down the barrel of Starr's six gun.

"That'll be enough," Captain Bowlin yelled from inside the house. "If you pull that trigger, Franklyn, you'll be dead before Duke John. Now, gather up your horse and clear out."

"Bowlin, I have a warrant for your arrest," Sheriff Wright interrupted.

"You heard me, Starr! If you don't put that gun away, we're going to fit you for a pine box."

I realized suddenly Captain Starr wasn't a coward, however he did qualify as a mean man and right then he wanted to kill me. I had gotten two bullets into his legs, and the man was still standing. How I don't know. He had some kind of determination which would not let him go down, but that same determination was holding me at gunpoint. He was mad! I had gotten two bullets into him and he had missed me altogether. The barrel of his six gun was growing ever larger in my eyes.

"Starr, don't make me shoot you."

"It's empty anyway." Slowly Captain Starr holstered his pistol.

Out of nowhere two men were beside the captain to help get Starr back up on his horse. He was game. If I hadn't known it before, I understood one thing now. If I

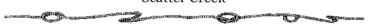

was going to kill Captain Starr, I had better do some practicing with my gun. I needed to find a way to get it into action faster and I needed to be more accurate. Flailing away with bullets doesn't accomplish a cotton pickin' thing. You're just spraying the countryside with lead with no chance of hitting your target. How I had escaped getting a bullet in me God only knows.

"Well Bowlin, are you going to surrender or not?"

"What am I being arrested for," Captain Bowlin shouted back.

"For burning down the Greene County courthouse."

"Sheriff, it might concern you to know that we are in the middle of fighting a war. How do you know the Yankee's didn't do it?"

"The Yankees have no interest in burning down courthouses, but vagrant criminals like you do," Sheriff Wright argued.

"You killed my brother Jesse, and my brother-in-law in just the last few weeks. I don't mean to offend you, but I think if I give myself up, I shall never make the Greene County jail."

"You going to sit here and argue, or get me to a doctor," Captain Starr complained. "I'm bleedin'."

"You can hold onto your britches for one minute Franklyn, he didn't hit any of your vitals," the sheriff asserted. "Well Captain, what will it be? If I ride away empty handed, I'll have the judge change your status to shoot on sight."

"You do that and I'll kill you."

Now I was still standing at the bottom of the steps on front of the porch, and I felt completely helpless. My gun was empty, or next to it, and this dispute was not getting

resolved. The sheriff didn't seem like he wanted to leave, yet Captain Starr was in a scramble to go. The one thing I couldn't help but notice was the fact I was exposed like no one else. If gunfire opened up now, I was a sitting duck and would likely be the first one shot.

Suddenly, I wondered where Bob Eubanks was. Had he tipped the sheriff of to our presence here, or had he missed the posse altogether? How had the sheriff known to look for Captain Bowlin here? Was he a good guesser, or had Bob told him where to look? It couldn't have been Bob, the sheriff had a warrant and there had not been enough time for Bob to relay our whereabouts and have the judge issue such a warrant. It had to be the devil's luck that Sheriff Wright and his posse was even in the area.

After a long pause the sheriff relented. "We'll be back Nathaniel Bowlin, and I don't care if you are fighting a war."

Spurring his horse, the rest of the men followed Sheriff Wright out of the yard headed back to Gainesville. As the dust settled the men in the house began to make their way outside onto the front porch. Captain Bowlin came out last and looked down at me.

"Let me see that pistol, Duke."

I drew my gun and handed it up to him. He spun the cylinder and checked my loads. "Just what I thought, it's empty. Boy, the next time you're in a gunfight, you make sure that your last shot gets the job done, otherwise you might not get another chance. It was only luck that Starr had emptied his gun as well."

Not waiting for me to do it, the captain re-loaded my pistol and handed the gun back to me. "In a war, you keep six bullets in your gun at all times, not five. If it was peace

time, I would think safety first as well, but Duke John this is a war we're fighting, and that one extra shot makes all the difference."

"Yes sir," I replied shoving my gun back into my holster.

"John, when Bob gets back, if he gets back, I want him here until my return. I'm riding back to the Pfeiffer farm to talk with Heinrich."

"We'll be right here sir, and be careful."

"You know me, I'll be back."

After Captain Bowlin rode out John Stone walked over and sat down next to me on the front porch steps. I had sat down to clean my pistol.

"That took nerve, Duke, but if it had been me I would have shot the man's horse the moment he decided to use the animal for a shield. The horse would have moved or it would have collapsed right there, it might even have fallen on him. Either way you would have gotten a clear shot at the man once the horse was out of the way."

"I'll keep that in mind for next time, but something tells me he isn't likely to seek cover like that next time we meet. I have a feeling he's going to wade right in shooting."

"He might at that, he's going to have plenty of time to think about what happened here today," John said.

Vern Truman had been in the corral and for the last ten minutes he had been checking it over making sure it was solid and reinforced. The last thing we needed was to have our stock run off in the middle of the night. As he came out from the corral he spoke to John. "The horses are secure, but I would still recommend one of us sleeping

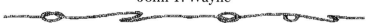

in the barn loft so that we have the corral covered in case anyone tries to get at them."

"Duke, why don't you take the loft," John said. "You'll have a good field of vision to cover the corral from up there, just be sure if something does happen that you don't shoot one of us and don't shoot the horses. It'll be dark all night. Take a loaded rifle with you."

Well, I don't mind doing my part, but I was once again filled with terror. What if I ran into a snake, a puff adder for instance? My nerves started shucking and jiving, looking for a place to hide, and you know what? There just wasn't anywhere. I had a job to do and nerves or not, I had to do it. I swallowed hard and walked out to the barn as the men looked on. I wanted a good long look at the stables in the daylight, with a good house cleaning upstairs before I lay my head down.

I had several hours before dark and I went through that barn with a fine tooth comb. I never found so much as a mouse. Snakes like mice, but if there aren't any, there are one or two answers as to why. Either the snakes are doing their job really good, or their just weren't any mice to be had. Having grown up in this part of the country, I can assure you, my conclusion was that the snakes were doing their job really good. That begged the question, where were they? I looked in every nook and cranny, but I never saw a reptile.

I sprinkled some hay under the open barn loft door just in case I had to make a blind jump in the middle of the night. I knew deep down in my gut if I got woke up next to a puff adder or any other kind of snake, there was going to be a sudden blind departure from the upper barn

loft door, and I wanted something down below to soften my landing.

Emile Haynes was occupying the rocking chair I had been sitting in when the posse rode into the yard. He was watching me from afar and then I saw him begin to laugh. He tugged on his pipe with a big smile and you know what? They could laugh all they wanted, I was not going to sleep with the snakes. I wanted the front porch, but on this night I had my duty.

Just before supper the men called me down and I washed up outside in the water barrel at the corner of the house. In those days a man kept an old whisky barrel at each corner of the house for fresh water what ran off the roof whenever it rained. Jesse's house had six barrels because it was an L shaped design with a wraparound porch. The system he had devised was genius to behold. When the barrels got so full, any additional runoff was transferred to the water troughs he had in place for the horses and mules.

As I finished washing up I took the hand towel hanging on the nail and dried off real good. I thought of Jesse then. His wife was still up in Missouri and I wondered, did she know what had happened? They had children, young ones if I was correct, and they would now be without a father.

I walked into the house and sat down at the makeshift table, all that was left after the place had been ransacked. All we had to eat was possum stew. I never was much on eating possum, but if it was cooked right, it was just as good as beef. A fellow couldn't tell much difference. In Green County Arkansas, possum was a delicacy for most

families during the war. You had to cook them with a lot of rice and beans, but tasted good when done right.

As I stabbed my spoon down into my bowl, I expected the worst flavor when I brought the spoon to my lips, but I was surprised by the aroma, Then I tasted it and I knew Wade Farley had taken some lessons on how to cook possum.

"The first one of you that complains about my possum grits is going to get shot," he declared.

I just dug in. I was starving. My bowl lasted about three minutes and I asked for more.

"Get what you want," Farley said. "A growing young lad like you has got to eat."

I got up and filled my bowl then returned to the table to put the possum grits right where they belonged, in my belly. Those fellows watched as I shoveled my second bowl down. They said nary a word, for they had been warned by the chef, but to my way of thinking, this particular pot of possum grits was one of the better ones I had tasted. When I finished my third bowl, John Stone said, "Duke, I ain't never seen anybody put away that much possum grits in my life."

"They ain't usually this good."

I picked up my things and scurried on out to the barn. Well, I had given them fellows something to talk about anyway. I made my bed near the barn loft door and I was out in no time. The entire Cherokee Nation could have ridden through and I wouldn't have heard a thing. I had slept so soundly that Bob Eubanks, who had returned from town after super, and Vern Truman were able to grab me by the arms and legs and toss me out the barn loft into the hay I had spread the evening before.

"That's for not waking up with the rooster," Bob called down from above.

I got up and dusted myself off, then I looked at my assailants.

"That's all right, your turn's coming," I said. I didn't do them the honor of looking their way any longer than necessary. I did, however, make a vow to myself that I was going to get even with both men as soon as the opportunity presented itself. "Teach them to pick on a sleeping young man," I mumbled as I walked toward the house for my share of breakfast.

Chapter 17

As I finished my late breakfast Captain Bowlin came riding into the yard. He dismounted and brought some good news. Zach Holmes was finally recovering and he was going to make it. We all smiled then, but our smiles didn't last long.

"We are going to ride over to Osceola and help a regiment on the river for a few days. I have word that Grant will be leaving Vicksburg now that it has fallen. He's returning to St. Louis and then reporting to Washington. I want to sink his boat."

We didn't waste any time. He had men coming to meet him, but he ordered John Stone and Bob Eubanks to stay at the house. He wanted to keep his brother's home intact. Everyone else, including me, rode out with Captain Bowlin an hour later. We hit the trail like we were running for our lives for the first ten minutes or so and then we settled in to a good distance eating cantor headed southeast through the swamp. Four tough men and a boy just learning the ropes.

My mount had been bringing up the rear. I was not on Jericho, for Captain Bowlin had borrowed a US branded horse from Mr. Pfeiffer in order for me to give Jericho a rest. He had noticed that my horse was beginning to limp again and knew how much the animal meant to me.

At noon the following day we neared the settlement of Osceola. Bowlin had word that Grant was steaming north

on an ironclad, named the *Benton*. We had word that this was Admiral Porter's flagship and Captain Bowlin was determined to disable it then blow her out of the water. Then he could apprehend General Grant along with Porter and deal a striking blow to the Yankee command. It sounded like a good plan, but what did I know? I had done some fighting, but how do you blow an ironclad out of the water? The few I had seen while in St. Louis seemed as if a cannon ball would bounce right off of them.

At Osceola there were two thirty pound cannons mounted on wheels and Captain Bowlin had no trouble enlisting the help of the artillery battery once he explained his mission. Capturing or killing Grant would deal a mighty blow to the plans the north had for conquering the rest of the south. With Grant on the loose, the north seemed to be having their way.

As we maneuvered the cannons into position, a boat came upstream with red crosses painted on her side. It was the *Graham*. I stood on the edge of the riverbank and watched as it made its way upriver. As I focused on the wheelhouse I became certain the pilot of the boat was Captain Grimes. I waved and the Confederate mail runner waved back. I wondered if he recognized me, but there was no doubt the bearded man was Grimes, the man who had rescued me from Ol' Slantface and the preacher several weeks earlier. I smiled with a bit of satisfaction knowing the captain was still alive.

"You know the captain?" Bowlin asked.

"Yes sir, Captain Grimes is the Confederate mail runner. He seems to be able to run the Yankee blockades at will."[4]

"But you seem to know him, how is that possible?"

"He freed me from being kidnapped not long ago. Ol' Slantface and the preacher Jeremiah Culpepper had me hogtied and chained to a barn wall. He set twenty seven boys free with a little help from his friends, some fellows calling themselves the Night Riders. I was one of those boys."

"What on earth were they doing kidnapping boys?"

"Their plan was to sell us aboard ship as cabin boys down New Orleans way. If it hadn't been for the captain, I'd be a slave aboard ship by now."[5]

"I see. You've had one hell of a year so far, haven't you."

"Yes sir, and I sure hope it gets better."

Captain Bowlin went to work then to set the cannons so that they could fire on the ironclad without hindrance. I never knew just what was involved in setting up a cannon until that day. I watched and learned.

First they set the things behind some rather large bushes so that the Yankee's wouldn't be able to see them right away. Then they cleared a slight spot through the middle of the bushes to create a good line of sight, the easiest of all cannon fire techniques. Once the cannons were in position they chocked the wheels so that the apparatus would not roll forward or backward from the concussion of the shot being fired. Then came the

---

4 Captain Grimes Mockingbird Lane Press 2015

5 Ol' Slantace Mockingbird Lane Press 2014

stacking of the ammo and gunpowder within easy reach. As set, the cannons were on the back side of an uphill embankment making them nearly impossible to hit.

"Now, if we're lucky, Grant and Porter will be under our guns for at least ten minutes," Bowlin stated.

No sooner had he finished when Wade Farley hollered, "There she comes!"

We all turned to see the *Benton* steaming upriver not far from our position. She was out in the middle of the river belching a full head of steam. The iron ship seemed even more menacing, only because I knew General Grant was on board. Grant had a way of laying waste to anything in his path, at least that seemed to be his reputation. I would later learn that was because of another general whom he relied upon named Sherman. A black-hearted soldier if there ever was one. His motto seemed to be, leave nothing behind, nothing the enemy can use, and kill all humans who get in the way.

The first two rounds were loaded and the cannons readied. Captain Bowlin told the gunners to be certain of their trajectory and mark their first shot. I didn't know what that meant, but the captain sure did. As the men readied the cannons, Captain Grimes sailed the *Graham* around the point ahead and slithered out of sight. Grant was that close to him and gaining it seemed. I held my breath hoping we could stall the *Benton* and provide Captain Grimes with a well-needed advantage.

"Fire one," Captain Bowlin shouted.

The cannon to my right belched and I watched as the ball split the water about fifty yards shy of the ironclad, but the round had been straight and true.

"Up one hundred," the gunner shouted as the powder monkey began shoving the next load of gunpowder down the barrel.

"Fire two," Captain Bowlin ordered and the other cannon played its song. The ball landed a little in front of the boat, but would have hit had it not been aimed too much to the left. Without hesitation I watched the other powder monkey get his cannon loaded before the first one. This was important, because if the boat continued to sail north, there was a good chance of hitting it broadside without having to move the cannon's trajectory, unlike the first cannon which would now be off a bit.

"Fire two," Captain Bowlin repeated and the cannon leaped once again. This time we scored a direct hit, but I watched the ball ricochet off the steel plating, screaming in another direction and eventually landing somewhere across the river.

"Is gun one set?"

"Yes sir," the gunner responded.

"Fire one," and the cannon danced once again. I watched as this time I was able to track the ball and it was another direct hit on the hull of the ironclad. Again, the cannon ball went whizzing off into the sky, bound for who knows where.

"We've got to hit her at the water mark or we'll never do any damage. Ready your cannons."

I watched as number two adjusted ever so slightly and then the gunner gave the ready signal. Suddenly a door opened up on the side of the craft and a cannon bellowed its retaliation. I knew instantly that we were in for a fight, because the cannonball landed directly on the

hill in front of us and exploded it seemed, throwing dirt, sand and debris all over everyone at our position.

"Good Lord almighty, she's packing forty pounders, captain," the gunner at the number one position said.

"Fire two," Captain Bowlin ordered and number two belched another iron ball. The smoke from our guns had given our position away, but if the Yankee's were going to get us they were going to have to destroy the entire hill in front of us. The ball hit the *Benton* square at the water line and men jumped and shouted, for the hit had done some damage.

Before we could celebrate too much the ironclad discharged another round which hit our position just as the ball before it, only this time it had been a little closer, and I began to get nervous. Those forty pounders packed quite a wallop and when they exploded they let you know they had landed. I began to look around for cover because I wasn't doing anything myself, I was just in the way here. If I didn't seek cover, I was likely going to pay a heavy price.

Noting a spot about ten yards behind me which was hollowed out at the base of a tree I walked back to it and dug in sort of. My plan was to get my head down low. There was no sense in getting my head blown off when it was completely unnecessary. Captain Bowlin looked back at me but didn't say anything, returning his attention to the task at hand.

"Fire one." Again the cannon on my right flowered and bounced as the cannonball ejected from the barrel headed for its target. I couldn't see where it landed and no longer cared to watch. In order to see I had to stand up, and for some reason the certainty of a forty pounder

finding me was the one thought I couldn't get out of my head.

Again I heard the ironclad respond and a moment later I heard something whistling overhead. The ball landed in the forest behind me, and I cringed at the thought of how close it had been. How could anyone survive being hit by one of those things? The answer came back to me simple, no one could!

"Fire two," Captain Bowlin commanded. Cannon number two lifted from the ground as the ball left the end of the gun and smoke belched from the barrel. I could see our guns firing, but there was nothing in me which wanted to watch those forty pounders being launched at our position. I heard the ironclad bellow once again and this time the cannonball ripped tree limbs from the tree I was nestled under. I had to duck in order to keep from getting hit. When I looked up, Bowlin was smiling at me like it was just another day in the park.

"Fire one," he yelled as he stared at me. "Are you all right back there, Duke?"

"I can't say."

"You get on back to the horses and mules, keep an eye on them, I don't want to lose even one of them by accident," he instructed me.

I was happy to oblige. We had tied the animals up about three hundred yards in the woods once we had the cannons set. There was little chance of a cannonball getting through all of the tall trees. I picked up my rifle and headed back, ducking behind a tree every time I heard one of those forty pounders fire. Good thing too, because the second time I ducked, the tree I ducked behind got hammered. It shook for what seemed like a

long time, little tree limbs falling all around me. When I looked up I could see where the ball had split the tree about two thirds of the way to the top. The ball was still wedged in the tree.

I took off running then, for I was out of sight of the gun position and I wanted out of reach. I seemed to me those cannons were seeking me out. The deeper I went into the woods, the deeper those balls seemed to penetrate the forest. I was not finding any sort of comfort with the sounding of those forty pounders. Then suddenly all fell silent.

I reached the animals and they were nervous, something I understood completely. Immediately I began to calm them. I had to in order to calm myself. The quiet was helping, and I went from one to another until I had them all gentled. Had I not arrived when I did, likely some of them would have gotten loose and run.

Waiting there in the silence, I wondered what had happened. Who had won? I couldn't see a thing. There was only silence and waiting. Then about ten minutes later, Haynes, Truman, and Farley appeared and told me to help them bring up the stock.

"What happened?" I asked.

"The boat eventually got too far upriver for us to hit it, and General Grant sailed away. He could have ordered Porter to pound our position once he was out of range of our guns, but he didn't. He must have other pressing matters than to trifle with the likes of us," Vern Truman stated.

We gathered the animals and headed down to the river. For fifteen minutes we worked to get the mules back in front of the cannons and then we stored the cannon

balls, what was left, on the company wagon and headed for Osceola. There was a storm coming and we could hear thunder in the distance, but we couldn't see through the thick forest of trees.

By the time we reached Osceola we were a sopping wet crew. From the talk on the way back, I didn't have to ask any questions. I was completely filled in by the time we arrived back in town. Most of the balls we had fired just bounced off the side of the ironclad and sailed away. Only one scored a hit at the waterline, and I had personally witnessed that one.

We put our animals away in the stables and found a small café on the town square. The rest of the day was spent eating, talking over coffee, and cursing our luck. Grant had sailed away unharmed. Our mission had failed to do any real damage at all, which was something Captain Bowlin was not used to. He was a regular practitioner when it came to raising hell with the Yankee's. Needless to say he was in a quiet mood as everyone else spoke of what had happened, what hadn't happened and what might have happened.

"Enough," Bowlin said raising his voice for all to hear. "Clearly we failed in our mission, and I don't like coming up on the short end, gentlemen. The next time we have an engagement, there had better be results."

We sat quiet for a while then, and just stared out the windows at the rain. With nothing else to do I thought it might be a good time to ask myself some questions, mainly, how long was it going to be before I could head west, and then what kind of shape would I be in when I did? My money was in the bank up St. Louis way, but half of it was likely to evaporate when the war ended. That in itself a bitter pill to swallow.

The other thing on my mind was physical condition. Would I be missing a leg, an arm, or an eye? It seemed to me that the war effort was getting dangerously close to Duke John Robinson. Bullets were flying, cannon balls were bouncing off trees and as time moved forward I was growing up, not yet a man, but getting awful close. If the war lasted two more years, I *would* be a man. I would no longer have an excuse to dodge the war. Fact is, I had no excuse now.

Captain Bowlin managed to arrange for us to stay in the loft at the stables down the street. The five of us bid our goodbye's to the artillery detachment and made our way down to the barn. It was wet and muddy, a miserable night in the Mississippi River Delta.

What is it about war that makes it seem so unreal? So far I had gone unscathed but for the death of my father, my luck undeniable. What was it Pa had always said, "Sometimes a fellow can't dodge trouble, even when he sees it coming right at him." Well, I had learned that lesson pretty well of late. Between the war and the efforts of the Starr family, I was lucky to be alive.

For the next twenty-one months in which I rode with Captain Nathaniel Bowlin, we were engaged in one fracas after another, but somehow Sheriff Wright left us alone. Captain Starr recovered and so did Bubba, and then it was mid-April 1865 and we learned that Lee surrendered to Grant at some place called Appomattox.

We were looking down on a Yankee Regiment from the crest of a hill in Missouri when the news came. In another hour we would have ridden into combat. I looked over at my captain and knew he was pricked in his heart. State's Rights would forever be trumped by the Federal

Government, and this did not correspond with the Constitution, nor with what the founding fathers had intended. War is the most severe form of censorship, for when you can no longer tolerate the other side, the next step is war.

"Well, men," he stated from his saddle. "We ride home on the morrow, and we will turn ourselves in at Pocahontas. The Yankee's possess the town and the land thereabouts."

I took stock of myself then, and I knew I would be heading west, just as fast as I could make the arrangements. I was now an even six feet tall. I weighed in about one eighty-five and my arms were bulging with muscle. I had grown up in the middle of a war. I could hop the back of my horse from a standstill, land right in the middle of the saddle and hit the ground running. I had learned this maneuver from Captain Bowlin.

I could get my pistol into action quicker than any man in the outfit, and I had practiced every day in order to accomplish it. I could hit a running doe at three hundred yards with a clear field of vision. I could cook somewhat, because I had paid attention, and I was pretty good with a rope, an axe, and a knife. I could shoot a slingshot better than most, and I could set a trap for any game. At seventeen, I had become self-sufficient.

Early on the men had a habit of kidding me and calling me squirt, but as I practiced with my pistol every day, that kind of talk soon subsided.

"How come you fellows don't call me squirt anymore," I asked one day.

"Well Duke, it's like this. I don't think any of the men in this unit wants to find themselves a target in front of

that pistol you're packing. They've been watching you and you're scaring them," Captain Bowlin assured me.

"What do you mean scaring them?"

"Duke, there ain't a man in Arkansas or Missouri that can pull iron as fast as you. On top of that, you hit what you aim at. Because of that, the men have decided to allow you a certain respect. Not one of them wants to be the hombre that makes you mad or ends up in front you."

I looked around the camp and suddenly I knew I would be all right. My friends, as they were, had accepted me and I was the youngest among them. I had come to them a kid and I had grown to be a man in two short years. If only Pa could see me now.

Two years had somehow gotten away from me. I thought suddenly of my siblings. I knew where they all were now, but I had not gathered them together because of circumstances. Maybe now that the war was over I could do something.

Chapter 18

When we got back to Arkansas we stopped at the Pfeiffer farm and visited with the folks there. As we ate supper that evening a morbid piece of news came riding into the yard along with Bob Eubanks who had detoured straight for home when the war ended. He lived near Pocahontas.

"Captain, I think we had better lay low."

"Why Bob, what's in the wind?"

"The Yankee's have burned several structures in Pocahontas, but they saved the St. Charles Hotel for their headquarters. The wire is still up and working. Yesterday was April 15th sir."

"So, what does April 15th have to do with anything?"

"The President was assassinated, sir. Abraham Lincoln is dead."

Bowlin's fork paused halfway to his mouth, then slowly lowered it back to his plate. "That means only one thing, gentlemen. This war ain't over yet."

"That's about how I figure, sir," Bob added.

"Have a seat Bob, we might as well think this through. If this war is over, it sure has a funny way of laying the wrong cards face up on the table."

"Sir, President Johnson is a southerner. Lincoln took him on in order to appeal more to the southern states, but even that seems too little too late," Eubanks offered.

"I agree, but with the death of Lincoln, there's no doubt he's the man in charge."

I looked around the dining room and realized for the last two years these men had been my friends. Captain Bowlin, John Stone, Bob, Emile Haynes, Vern Truman, and Wade Farley. We had all survived the war together, and now it appeared that we might just be going right back to war. I sat in the corner chair while the older men gathered around the table and talked, those I just mentioned, along with Henrick Pfeiffer.

The fact was I had grown up, but I wanted nothing more than to go back to my childhood right then. I wanted my father back and I wanted my brother and sisters back, but I knew deep down inside that wasn't about to happen. Life had gone too far and there was no going back. I couldn't do anything about my father, and who knew what had become of my siblings. I knew where they all were now, but had yet to see them.

About sundown a woman came riding in on a white mule. She presented herself as Belle Starr. This got my attention right away. I knew the Starr family, and yet I couldn't place her. There was Bubba, Jupiter and Asa, but as far as I knew, Franklyn had no daughters. After she ate I asked Mrs. Pfeiffer if I could enquire about my brother and sister. She brought me to the parlor with the idea to let me see what the young woman knew.

"Ma'am, my name is Duke John Robinson. My sister and brother were at the Starr ranch the last time I was by the place. I'm wondering if you might know of their condition," I asked.

"So, you're Duke John Robinson." She stared at me for a long time and then added, "You don't look anything like a runny nose kid to me."

"Ma'am?"

"Captain Starr insists that you're nothing more than a runny nose kid. Now, that may have been true a couple of years ago, but I don't see where he can possibly be talking about the young man I'm looking at right now."

"Kids grow up," I said.

"Yes they do," she replied looking me up and down.

She was homely looking, but she had a good figure and she was packing a mighty big pistol in a holster around her fringed dress."

"Do you always carry a pistol like that," I inquired.

"In times like these a young lady had better go armed," she said.

"Duke, would you like to join us for some tea," Mrs. Pfeiffer asked.

"I haven't had any tea in a long time. If the young lady don't mind, ma'am," I said looking directly at Belle Starr.

"Well now, why would I mind the company of such a fine young man," she said as she looked me up and down again. Her stare was making me rather uncomfortable. I hadn't been around women folk much of late.

I walked over to a chair and sat down while Mrs. Pfeiffer fussed with a tea tray.

"Ma'am, I grew up in the De'Laplaine swamp and I don't recall the Starr family having a daughter, especially one my age," I said.

There was no mistaking my meaning and Mrs. Pfeiffer winced as she poured the last cup of tea. She must have thought there was about to be a gunfight right there in her parlor, but Belle Starr was not intimidated.

"Duke John, you haven't been around much lately. The Starr family adopted me a few years ago. My real name was Myra May Belle Shirley, but I like the name

Starr and I have accepted it. If you don't mind, I think I'll keep it."

"Makes no difference to me, but the Federals might have other ideas," I stated.

Mrs. Pfeiffer handed me a cup of tea and we all sipped from our cups then. No one said anything for a few minutes, but after our cups were empty, Myra May Belle Shirley picked up the conversation once again. "Captain Starr is real put out with you, Duke. He said he's going to kill you on sight," she explained.

"He might, but I'll make sure he gets a few chunks of lead to remember me by."

"Oh, he's already got that," she said. "In fact, he's got them laying on the fireplace mantle and he looks at them every day right along with the bullet that they took out of Bubba. Like father like son, they both plan to kill you."

"And you?"

"I'm not in the fight. I'm just a drifter," she stated matter of fact.

"That piece you carry is bigger than any gun most men carry," I said.

"A gun this big is a deterrent. It keeps men from getting too sentimental when they start sparking me. Keeps their hands off me. I don't like being pawed by no greasy man who hasn't had a bath," she added.

"Hadn't thought of things quite in that respect, but you'd be right. I sure wouldn't bother you none."

With my statement she got a sudden look of disappointment on her face and developed a frown. I could see that maybe I had hurt her feelings and then I did something I still can't explain, not even to this day.

"Ma'am, would you care to take a walk with me?"

"I'd be delighted, Duke."

I stood up and so did Myra. She unbuckled her gun-belt and laid it on the chair, so I did likewise. I looked over at Mrs. Pfeiffer and she was a bit disappointed that she was losing her company, but she understood. Walking through the dining room we passed by the men who were still engaged in discussions about the assassination of President Lincoln and what such an event might mean for the peace effort. I would like to make a note here that when April 15th rolled around the following year and every year since, is the day that the Yankee's chose for retribution. To one and all April 15th has become the Federal Government's annual tax day!

In just a short time the government had figured out how to take more money from the American people than they could ever possibly spend, and then they proceeded to spend more money than they could ever possibly collect. Now, I would like to clarify my belief about America. I love my country, but every once in a while it seems that the Federal Government has to show its back side to the American people.

On the front porch I stepped down the stairs in front of her while she followed. Once out in the front yard we headed toward the large willow tree on the northeast corner of the property. As we neared the tree, Myra May Belle Shirley asked me what it was like to be in a gunfight.

"Well, Myra, I can assure you this much, it isn't fun and games. You don't have time to think, you just become reactionary and all you can hope for is that you're faster and more accurate than the man facing you."

"What do you mean faster? Don't you walk off ten paces then turn and shoot?"

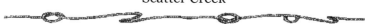

"That would be a duel and that would be much more preferable than having to drag iron without notice, but Myra, men have changed. This war has changed them. I think the days of dueling are over for the most part. Any grievance a man settles now will be done swiftly and without a monitor. There won't be anyone calling off ten paces and supervising the event. If a duel happens now, it will be off the cuff. The war has gotten everyone to where no one trusts the other. Nope, if a duel happens now, it will be an all-out gunfight with little or no warning," I promised her.

"Maybe I had better start practicing with my shooting iron," she said.

"You're a woman, what in the world do you need to practice for?"

"That's right, I am a woman, but I sure don't intend to let no man get the drop on me."

"I can't ever imagine an instance where any man would pull a gun on a woman," I argued.

"I can. If you don't mind I think I'll just set out to get a little practice."

"No man is ever going to get into a gunfight with you, not unless he wants the nickname of sissy," I told her.

"Just the same, a woman wants to know she has some security, so I think I'll just work on getting my gun into action swiftly."

"Something a little smaller would help," I chided.

I just stared at her for a moment then and wondered what kind of woman she was. I had never met anyone like her, a woman packing iron in a holster. She had the most soothing voice, and I thought what she didn't have in the

way of looks, she made up for with her voice and other features.

Then suddenly she said to me, "Sarah misses you, and so does your brother Dwayne."

"What are they doing at the Starr Ranch, I left them with some folks in Gainesville when Pa disappeared."

"Well, they had to live somewhere. The Starr family is as good a place as any. They ain't hurt none."

"But Captain Starr and Bubba seem to hate me. They want to kill me. You said that just a few minutes ago. How can it be good for them to hear such things?"

"I don't have an answer for that, but I do know they miss you regardless of what Captain Starr says."

"What are your plans," I asked out of the blue.

"I thought I would head for Carthage, Missouri. There's a girl's school there and I've been accepted. I've been told more than once I could stand to learn some manners."

"Might do you some good, but don't go forgetting who you are Myra May Belle Shirley."

"You know, Duke, a woman could get used to being around a man like you."

"I've got to side Captain Bowlin a little longer, but when the war is for sure over, I plan to head west."

"You plan on leaving these parts?"

"I do. I want to see the west and the big sky out there. I've heard it goes on forever."

Without warning Myra took my right arm, turned me to face her and kissed me right on the lips. My reaction was to jump back and stare at her for a long silent moment.

"What's the matter, am I a scary-to-death woman?"

"No, no, I just wasn't expecting something like that, that's all."

"Surely you know that you're handsome."

"I haven't had time to think about what I look like," I answered. "I've been fighting this stupid war."

"You think this war is stupid?"

"No. I think the reason behind this war is stupid. The men who can't come to terms with one another and causing so much death and destruction, that is what I think is stupid. War is the most extreme form of censorship. When you can no longer persuade your enemies, you eliminate them."

"I hadn't really thought about it."

"You're not alone, most men don't think about such things."

"You're going to be somebody, Duke John Robinson. Don't ask me how I know such a thing, I just do."

Myra May Belle Shirley rode out the following morning on her way to Carthage. I felt sorry for any gent who set his mind on her, because my feeling was that Myra could take care of herself in any situation. In any room she was in, I could bet she was the one in charge. I just couldn't see her any other way.

For the next six weeks I kept my head low and settled in at Jesse Bowlin's old home. This was done with Captain Bowlin's graces, because he didn't want to see the place torn up. The one thing I did manage to do was go to Peach Orchard and get my wolf hound. I didn't have any visitors those first six weeks and then one day Bob Eubanks came riding in. He unsaddled his horse, let it drink from the trough out front then led it to the corral, Joker barking the entire time, although from a distance.

Turning to me, I was sitting in the rocking chair on the front porch, he said, "Duke, do you know where to find Captain Bowlin?"

"I believe he's up at his place in Missouri."

"Don't go getting any ideas about surrendering to the Federal troops over at Pocahontas. They just murdered seven men from Wayne County, Missouri."

"What do you mean murdered?"

"Once they had surrendered, their hands were bound behind their back, they were blindfolded, marched outside, and shot dead."

My heart started pounding. There was nothing I could do about it. For a minute I thought it would leap from my chest. What did those Yankee's think they were doing? The war had ended with Lee's surrender, but apparently not completely. Skirmishes were happening all around the countryside, but the act Bob had just described was hideous. How could the Yankee's murder seven unarmed helpless men, men who had surrendered peacefully?

"If you don't mind, I'll stay the night with you, Duke, and ride out in the morning. Captain Bowlin needs to hear about this first hand."

"Well, tell him Morris Wright is still gunning for him. He's been talking it up all over the county what he plans to do when he runs into Captain Bowlin."

"I'll tell him, Duke. I'd like to be there when the captain rides in. I don't think Sheriff Wright has the nerve to tackle Nathaniel Bowlin head on."

"I hope you're right, but he's a mean one. He's got everybody in the county afraid to move, afraid to call out his name, or to simply even speak to him."

"You got some coffee?"

"I do, but it will take about a half hour to get some ready. Come on in the house," I said. "We can talk in there."

Getting up from my chair we entered the house and I grabbed the coffee pot off the table. I threw the old grounds out the back door and rinsed out the pot. Then I dipped the pot full of water in the rain barrel at the corner of the house. Back at the kitchen table I added fresh coffee grounds and then put it on the open flame in the fire place. I wouldn't even have had a fire going, but the morning had been a chilly one so I had re-stoked it rather than let the flame die out completely.

"Bowlin isn't going to like this news at all," Bob said.

"I don't know anyone who would," I added.

"Duke, you be careful. If you have to go to town, ride down to that new settlement Parmalay or somewhere else, don't go to Gainesville. Starr is just waiting for you to ride over that way."

"I still have to gather my brother and sisters. I promised Pa I would make sure we all made contact before I took off west."

"You be careful doing it. There's no love lost between you and Franklyn Starr."

"I'll be careful. I got nothing better to do," I promised.

The following morning Bob rode out and I began to tidy things up around the house. Not that I hadn't been doing so already. I had to keep myself busy and the place needed a lot of work. Jesse's place had been neglected the last several years. First I cleared the encroaching grass from the yard and pulled a few weeds. Then I got out the rake and raked the entire yard to clear it of debris such as

small twigs and pine cones. I put all of that in a box by the front door to use for kindling.

When finished, there was plenty to do inside the house. I dusted a few shelves which seemed to need dusting at least once a week. There was precious little food in the house to live on and for the last six weeks I'd been shooting my own breakfast, lunch, and supper. At times one kill would last a few days, at others I had to shoot something three times a day. Rabbit, squirrel, and turtles don't go very far, but a good size turtle makes for a good turtle stew, and you don't even need a pot, you can turn it upside down and cook it in a natural bowl just like that. The turtles make a pretty good stew when you add wild onions and potatoes. In a pinch I could rustle up some poke salad.

I was out of flour, grits, and cornmeal, so there wasn't any bread to bake. I had to live off the land, but this wasn't my first attempt. I was just lucky those soldier boys up in Missouri didn't come down to the Arkansas swamps very often. There was still plenty of wild game to be had in the swamps down below Crowley's Ridge.

I finished inside the house and went back to sit on the front porch. One thing I liked about this home was the sunset, and again a beautiful evening began to unfold.

I heard a horse coming up the road in the distance, a horse which kept hesitating. Being cautious of mind, I slipped the thong from my six-shooter and picked up my loaded rifle. The rifle had been lying against the porch railing, and I placed the full length across my lap. Slowly, with several interruptions, the horse continued up the road. As the rider came into view, I could see it was my younger brother, now fifteen. He looked full grown in the

saddle, maybe an inch or two taller than me, but I knew how old he was.

"Dwayne, am I glad to see you," I hollered as I stood up and put my rifle down.

"That's strange, because I'm here to settle a score," he said, and with no warning at all he dragged iron and started shooting at me.

"What are you doing," I yelled as I ducked behind a front porch post.

A bullet tore splinters from the post right by my head and suddenly I couldn't see. I was blind! With no recourse but to defend myself I pulled my pistol and began firing in the direction of my brother. I couldn't see a thing and expected a bullet in my head at any moment, but instead I heard one of my bullets strike something with a dull thud and I stopped firing.

"Dwayne," I yelled, "are you all right?"

There was no answer. I rubbed at my eyes but it only made matters worse. I could see nothing. I holstered my pistol and made my way down off the front porch, feeling my way down by rail. Slowly I made my way over to where I knew the horse to be. There on the ground lay my brother, and he was dying. I had shot him right through the chest. Dropping to my knees I pulled his head into my lap and fought through the blurriness in my eyes.

"What were you doing? Why were you trying to kill me," I cried.

"You killed Pa," he whispered back.

"Franklyn Starr killed our Pa two years ago," I said.

Dwayne's eyes lit up with realization and then he was gone. There was naught I could do to save him. My eyes were burning from the wood splinters and my heart was

torn into. Not like Cain had killed Abel, but in self-defense. I was torn to shreds internally. How could this be? What kind of God would let something like this happen? Suddenly, I began to curse God!

Chapter 19

Two days later as I stood over my brother's grave, I found myself ashamed. "Lord," I prayed. "I know this was none of your doing, for you're not of evil, but love. This was the work of Satan, and I'm ashamed of how I've behaved. I'm sorry. You didn't cause this to happen, it was set up by evil men. Lord, you say "vengeance is mine," but I pray if you will allow me at all, let me be the instrument of your vengeance. Let me provide the wrath for what has happened here. I know that you use men to do your work, and all I'm asking is for you to let me be that man. Amen."

I went back to the house. Either Franklyn Starr was going to meet his maker, or I was. My mind was made up. Somehow he had tricked my brother into believing that I had killed our father when in fact, it had been Captain Starr himself. What he was captain of still remained to be seen, for he had not fought in the war at all.

I gathered my mojo bag and sat down in the rocking chair once more. Leaving my pistol loaded, I removed the thong and then began to empty my rifle. Once it was empty, I started breaking it down for a good cleaning. I wanted the action working perfectly with no chance of dirt mucking up the works. I was fixing to kill me a no account from way back down the pike.

I labored over my rifle for more than an hour, then I reloaded it and leaned it against the porch railing as before. Slipping my pistol from its holster I emptied it and began to break it down. I wanted it clean as well. When I

215

was finished, I cleaned the pistol my brother had used on me. Then I strapped on the other belt and dropped the pistol in place. It was backward, but I knew I could get another holster which was designed for a left hip.

Next I took the rifle my brother had kept in his scabbard. Unloading the weapon, I began to clean one more time. It was late afternoon before I realized I had not eaten in hours. There was a squirrel in the tree across the way so I raised my brother's rifle to my shoulder and took aim. Squeezing the trigger, I saw the squirrel go flying. I lay the rifle down and went to pick it up. Not only had the squirrel been my supper, that squirrel had been target practice, and the target had been Franklyn Starr.

When morning came I heard the horses coming down the road. From the direction they were heading I knew it was likely Captain Bowlin and company, but to be safe I slipped into the house so I could watch from the front window. As the horses came into view, I relaxed for it was them.

Stepping out onto the front porch I waited. The horses gathered around, but first they looked things over.

"That grave wasn't there when I left," Captain Bowlin said.

"No sir, but it is now."

"What happened," Bowlin wanted to know, so I told him. "Captain Starr sent my brother to kill me," and that was all I could say without tearing up.

"Of all the rotten things for a man to do, Duke, are you ready to set things straight?"

"Yes sir, but he still has my little sister."

"Don't worry, we'll catch him in town."

I was choking back tears and the men could see it. My friends for the last two years were there to witness my trauma. John Stone, Bob Eubanks, Emile Haynes, Vern Truman, Wade Farley, and the captain. I fought back the tears, but my eyes watered up anyway. I wasn't bawling, but the tears were still forcing their way through.

The men got down and unsaddled their horses, laying their saddles here and there on the front porch. Then one by one they led the animals into the corral. I took my perch in the rocking chair and my friends didn't bother me for a long time. Once in a while one of them would step onto the front porch and roll a smoke, just to check on me it seemed. I was still in a state of shock for having buried my own brother, for having to shoot him as well. Nothing in my countenance seemed stable. I lifted my pistol and rolled the cylinder in my hand. It was loaded with six bullets.

"Shooting yourself ain't going to bring your brother back, Duke." It was Vern who spoke. He had been leaning against the front porch railing smoking a fresh rolled cigarette.

"I don't figure on shooting myself," I replied. "I'm thinking about that evil snake what calls himself Captain Starr." Again I spun the cylinder then dropped the gun back into my holster. "I don't figure on dying without taking him with me," I added.

"That's good to know. I thought maybe you were thinking about something else."

"Not hardly," I answered with disdain.

"Don't worry, we'll be there to back you up," Vern said.

"I won't need any. I'm going to just let him have it."

"We'll be there just the same. I think Captain Bowlin is ready to avenge Jesse's death as well."

"I'm not sure I understand you."

"Let's just say if you or Captain Bowlin either one goes down, there are friends to spirit you away."

"I may be up against Starr, his three sons and his ranch foreman all at once. I'm not coming away from that without taking lead. I'm just going to make sure I kill the big rat first. He sent my own brother after me. Then I'm going to get as many of the others as I can before they get me."

"We'll be right there beside you, Duke."

I knew these men, I knew them from riding all over the countryside with them in the middle of a war. They would stand, and they would fight. It wasn't their fight, but yet it was. We had been through a lot together, and none of them had any intention of letting me go it alone, or Captain Bowlin for that matter.

I eased myself in my rocker and closed my eyes. I had me some friends. Good friends who would not let me ride into an ambush alone. An ambush is what I figured they would lay for me, simply because if I was in their shoes, I would lay one for them. I had no other evidence in the matter, but the feeling was strong. There would be someone lying in wait, and if I killed Starr, it would be their task to shoot me down. I was playing with hellfire, but I had to avenge my brother and father.

The following morning we saddled up and rode out, and just so there would be no misunderstanding what had happened, I rode my brother's horse. Dwayne's horse had the Starr brand on it, and everybody would know where I got my mount, especially Franklin Starr.

My eyes were still sore from getting splinters in them a few days earlier, but they were settling down. While they were still irritated, I could see fine. Once again Captain Bowlin had suggested I side him as we made our way to Gainesville, the county seat.

The ride had been a long two hours, but we had not been in a hurry. Our reasoning was we wanted to give Starr a chance to arrive in town if he was coming. If not, we'd go get him after taking care of Sheriff Wright. That was the plan, but when we rode down the hill into town it our carefully laid plans blew up in our faces.

Somehow we made it all the way down to Osteen's store before there was any sign of trouble. Captain Bowlin dismounted from his horse and stepped up to the front porch steps. Just then the front door opened and Sheriff Wright stepped out with his hands full. Before anyone could react, Sheriff Wright swore and dropped his parcel, his hand sweeping down for his gun as he did so. Captain Bowlin was at a disadvantage because he was down lower than the sheriff, but his gun swung up and blossomed once, twice, and then a third time. Suddenly the sheriff squeezed his trigger and his pistol barked in return. His gun slipped from his hand as he dove back inside the building.

Vern and John helped Captain Bowlin onto his horse and we lit a shuck for Jesse's cabin. Captain Bowlin had been hit, but as of yet we had no idea how bad. If my eyes hadn't deceived me, the sheriff had taken three of my captain's bullets. We rode like bandits, but it was broad daylight and soon we rode into the yard at the cabin.

John Stone and Bob Eubanks helped Captain Bowlin into the house, and I went to unsaddling their horses. In

about five minutes we had the saddles removed and the men started taking up positions of a defensive nature, all of them on the lookout for a posse of some sort. I took this as a signal to take up my position in the barn loft, which I did while making certain there were no snakes. I hadn't forgotten about them.

At two in the afternoon a man came to the house and said he was to see if Captain Bowlin would in fact turn himself in. He was hurt badly, but his wound was not fatal. He replied in fact that he would turn himself in just as soon as he could travel.

The news was that Sheriff Wright had left the Osteen store and made his way to his home on the edge of town where he fell dead just inside his own front door.

Captain Bowlin's assurance was good enough for the man who had come to inquire, and he rode away after only a short visit inside the house.

I was on alert for any movement in the woods surrounding the house, the sound of a horse, a mule, or even a wagon. Somehow we had managed to get through the entire war effort without being shot, and now that it was supposed to be over, we were no longer so lucky. This did nothing to comfort me, for I still had a date with a rat named Starr.

Dr. Webb arrived as the sun went down and went to work on Captain Bowlin. I heard sounds of pain then, but I kept a lookout from the loft. I knew my friends were holding him down while the doctor cut on him. The war had taken most all of the laudanum or anything else which might help. Captain Bowlin was on his own as far a pain was concerned. Thinking of that made me wonder; was I next?

For three days we kept a low profile. Several folks from town had visited, and we heard he had resigned a few moments before the shooting took place, thus saving Captain Bowlin from killing an active duty sheriff. Not that it would have mattered. There were enough witnesses to support Bowlin's story that Wright had went for his gun first. Only luck had allowed Captain Bowlin to get the first three shots off.

All three days I gathered information and replayed the gunfight in my head, for I knew there was still one more to go. One more gunfight and it was mine. Would my friends stand beside me like they did the captain?

At noon that fourth day, I climbed down from the loft to get something to eat, just in time to hear horses coming up the road. It sounded like three or four, and I almost went back to the loft, but stopped just inside the barn door and waited.

It was Captain Starr and Bubba, along with Van Cleve. They circled their horses in front of the porch and commenced to yelling. "Where's that Robinson boy? I'm here to arrest him."

"I'm right here, captain," I said as he swung his horse around. He didn't give me a chance to say anything else he just pulled his six-gun and started talking with bullets.

I didn't stand by there to see if he could hit a stationary target or not. I stepped to the right and shucked my own pistol. At that moment I saw bodies diving everywhere. Bubba dove behind the water tough near the front porch like the coward he was. Van Cleve spurred his horse to get around the back of the house because he had been facing the wrong way when Starr opened up on me. Vern dove back inside the front door

having been caught in an unexpected crossfire when I commenced to shooting.

I drilled Captain Starr with no less than four slugs before he got one into me. His horse was dancing all over the place making it impossible for him to take aim. As for me, I aimed on purpose. This man had destroyed my family. I felt the slug rip at my left shoulder and then I felt the warm blood, but I put two more bullets into him as he struggled to stay on his dancing horse.

As he wavered back and forth on his mount I shucked my brother's gun and took aim. "One last bullet," I said. As I squeezed the trigger a blue hole develop in his forehead. His hat hit the ground and I saw the sheriff's badge. It was dented up real bad, but one of my bullets had not gone any further. The rest of my shots had been dead on. Starr slipped to the ground in a heap.

Now, Jesse Bowlin's house was on the old stage road, what was called Sawmill Road. As the dust began to settle I heard the stage coming down the ridge in the distance. The stage driver who hadn't been running of late, in fact not for almost four years because of the war, pulled to a stop in the yard.

A man in a black broadcloth suit exited the stage post haste and looked around. "What the devil is going on here? I heard gunfire."

My brother's pistol was still smoking, as was mine, the one I had dropped back into my right holster. "A gunfight," I said.

"Let me have those guns, young man."

Well I just looked at him like he was crazy. Bubba was still down behind that trough and Van Cleve was still

armed. "I'm not handing over anything until I know it's safe to do so."

"I said hand over your guns." Turning his head back to the stage he added, "Driver, if anyone moves you have my permission to shoot them down."

"Yes sir," the driver said as he picked up his shotgun.

"Now son, hand over your guns."

"First you're going to tell me who you are," I said. "I'm not giving up my guns what they don't give up theirs," pointing to Bubba and Van Cleve who was peaking around the corner of the house.

"The name is Judge Isaac Parker. I'm the new Federal Judge bound for Davidsonville. Now, you want to hand over those guns or do I have to take them from you?"

Well, the term Federal got my attention right away and I knew I was in some kind of trouble. I handed him both of my pistols and he looked them over. Before saying a word he handed them back to me.

"You ought to have someone take a look at that shoulder," he advised.

I hadn't even noticed I was hit, but suddenly I began to hurt. Starr had put a bullet into my left arm.

Turning, he saw Captain Starr was dead. Walking over to the body he flipped him over and stepped back. Turning to face me he said, "This man is a sheriff!"

I could see the consternation in Judge Parker's wrinkled forehead. He was a rather young fellow to be a Federal Judge. He was struggling with something almighty troubling. I could see it in his eyes. "What's your name, young man?"

"Duke John Robinson, sir."

"You ever been to the St. Louis orphan asylum young man?"

"Just to get a bite, sir."

"That's where I've seen you. You sat through some classes of mine."

When he said that, I realized his face had a familiar look to it. Then, like a long lost friend from the past I remembered. "You taught the class on law."

"That I did, but I'm wondering if my classes did any good. How did you come to kill the sheriff?"

I looked over to the stage driver and he had things well in hand so I began to explain the best I could. "That man on the ground is Captain Starr, he killed my father, sent my own brother to kill me and he just now tried to kill me with the help of Van Cleve and Bubba," I said pointing at them.

"Is that true, young man," he asked of Bubba who was crawling out from behind the trough.

"Depends, depends on how you look at it," Bubba said as he dusted off his pants.

"Let's try looking at it through the eyes of the law," Parker admonished.

"I suppose that Duke would be correct, but Pa was the sheriff. You can't kill a sheriff and get away with it," Bubba argued.

"Did he have a warrant for your arrest, Duke John?"

"If he did, he didn't say anything. Captain Starr just turned his horse and dragged iron when he saw me."

By now everyone who had been in the house was standing on the front porch watching the proceedings, everyone but Captain Bowlin who was laid up in the back room.

"Is that right, he just dragged iron?"

"That's what it looked like from here," Vern offered from the front porch.

Bending down Judge Parker started going through the coat pockets on Captain Starr. He finally stood up and looked around.

"Who are you?" he asked of Van Cleve.

"My name is Rufus Van Cleve. I'm the foreman at the Starr ranch."

"What are you doing here?"

"Excuse me?"

"You heard me, what are you doing here. If the sheriff was serving a warrant, what did he need his ranch foreman for? Enlighten me."

"Well sir, we..." Van Cleve trailed off with the realization that anything he said might lead to charges against him or Bubba. He stood there stone faced.

"I see. Some of you men load the captain onto his horse." Turning to Bubba he said, "What's your name, son?"

"Bubba."

"That's a nickname. I want your real name."

"My real name is Delta Starr, that's my father," he said pointing in the direction of Captain Starr who was being tied to his horse.

"All right, Bubba, I want to see you and you," he said pointing to Van Cleve, "in the house. I might as well start my inquisition here and now." Turning to the stage coach he told the driver to stand down. Then he walked over and spoke to someone inside the coach before entering the house.

I shucked my spent cartridges and began to reload my guns. I had learned one thing during the war, and that

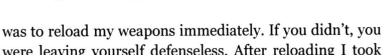

was to reload my weapons immediately. If you didn't, you were leaving yourself defenseless. After reloading I took up my brother's gun and replaced the one empty chamber. Dropping the pistol back into place I looked around and sighed.

All of this killing the last few days had been completely unnecessary—from the killing of my brother to the killing of Sheriff Wright and now Captain Starr. If the stage hadn't rolled in when it did, there would have been two or three more dead bodies, maybe even mine. The appearance of the stage had been the only reason the shooting had stopped.

I had taken a good look at Captain Starr and thought to myself, there just wasn't much blood on him, not for all the bullets I put into him. Then it occurred to me, a dead man wouldn't bleed. At some point, one of my bullets sent him packing and the others were shot into a dead carcass, including the last one which had hit him in the head.

Vern stepped out to me and said, "Why don't you take a seat in the chair on the front porch. I've sort of gotten used to seeing you there and from the looks of things this judge is a thorough fellow. It might be a little while before the stage leaves."

As I took my place in the old rocker I noted a fine young lady getting out of the stagecoach. Turns out she was the judge's secretary and wife. She took a large black leather case into the house and disappeared from sight. I began to rock back and forth as I had become accustom to the chair of late. Not that I was an old man, but I was trying to get comfortable, something which might end in short order—my comfort that is.

Chapter 20

My head was spinning as I tried to rest in the rocker, yet in a few minutes the men came out of the house except for Bubba. Only the wounded Nathaniel Bowlin was allowed to remain in the house. The inquisition had begun. I tried without result to ease my apprehension for what I knew was to come. I was going to have to give my own statement to the judge when called. This, I can tell you, made me more than just a little nervous.

I had put six bullets into the captain, seven if you counted the bent up star which captured one bullet. I was pleased with my shooting ability, and the fact I hadn't been fatally wounded. Remembering just then I had been wounded I took a look at my arm. My shirtsleeve was torn, and I had bled a good bit, but with everything happening around me, I had completely forgotten about being shot.

Dr. Webb walked to me and placed his black bag on the front porch beside me. "I didn't realize you were hit, Duke. Otherwise I would have attended to you already."

"It's all right, Doc, I don't think it's life threatening."

"No, but you need to let me treat you, otherwise you're wound could become infected," he stated.

With no further argument from me, Dr. Webb went to work on my arm. He cut open my left sleeve at the shoulder and began to clean the wound. I had bled a little and my entire shirt sleeve had turned crimson red. That I

had about forgotten being shot meant I wasn't hurt too bad. Rather than fuss with my bloody shirt sleeve any longer, Dr. Webb took up his scissors and cut the remainder from my arm altogether, dropping the bloody mess onto the front porch.

"That was my only shirt, Doc."

"Well then, its time you had a new one."

He pulled a leather strap from his bag and said, "Bite down on this. That bullet went deep and I've got to pull it out."

I bit down on the leather strap and immediately knew what pain was. He didn't even give me time to get set when he stuck a long pair of scissors with grips on the end right down into my arm. He started rummaging around in there causing more pain than when the bullet first entered. I kept my bite on the leather strap, but I was squirming as well.

Doc was slow and deliberate, making sure he got a good hold on the bullet before he began to pull the lead ball to the surface of my skin. I must have been squirming some, because he said, "Hold still, Duke."

I got news for you. Being told to hold still while a doctor is rooting around inside your shoulder is like being asked to hold your foot on a hot fire while you watch it sizzling. Your natural inclination is to pull your foot out of the fire, no matter what the doctor might say. My squirming beneath him in the chair was no different.

"There we go," he said as he lifted the bullet from my arm.

I spit the leather strap from my mouth and said, "Gee whiz, Doc, did you leave me an arm?"

He bent down and picked up the strap I had extricated from my mouth and stuffed it back in, "I'm not done yet."

Suddenly I was screaming in pain once again. This time he talked as he rooted around in my arm with his tool. "I've got to make sure and get all of the lead out of your arm, or else I'll be taking it off at the shoulder." He stuck me a few more times and I felt him strike bone then began to squeeze to get the contaminated blood out of my shoulder while I gritted my teeth in pain. "Next time somebody starts shooting at you, duck."

I looked over to see Bubba come out the front door and walk over to Van Cleve. Bubba said something to the foreman who turned and went inside the house. Everyone else was laughing and smiling while the doctor did his best to make me thoroughly uncomfortable. Finally Dr. Webb pulled the leather from my mouth and said, "I think that ought to do it. Now all I have to do is sew the wound shut. It's going to hurt a little, but nothing like what I just did."

He put three stitches in me and cut them so they wouldn't be a problem. "Come see me if this starts to turn red, if you see red streaks in your arm, or you get a fever. That's a sign of infection and that could be serious. Don't wait if that happens. You get to me as soon as possible, otherwise you could lose your arm, or worse."

"Is that all?"

"If it heals up all right, come see me in about two weeks and I'll remove those stitches for you."

"Thanks, Doc." I wanted to say more, but I held my tongue. I couldn't possibly imagine what I had to say

would be taken in good humor, so I figured it was better left unsaid.

I watched as Dr. Webb packed up his black bag of tricks and settled down on the front porch steps. He wasn't going anywhere, and then I remembered the judge inside getting his statements from everyone. I could only hope that I had someone on my side, or else I was fixing to hang for shooting a sheriff.

After a bit Van Cleve came out the front door and gave me one of those if-looks-could-kill stares, then made his way down the steps and got on his horse. He took the reins of Captain Starr's mount and turned to Bubba. "Come on, we're through here." A few of my friends had taken the time to load Starr onto his mount.

Bubba stepped into the stirrup and the two of them rode down the lane leading Captain Starr's horse. A couple of times Bubba looked back at me to stare for a moment, but then turned his attention forward. I watched as they rode away headed for Gainesville. They seemed a dejected lot, but then what did I know.

John Stone was the next man to enter the house and after about twenty minutes he came back out. Looking around the yard he motioned for Vern Truman and Vern entered the house next. For three hours the judge questioned everyone but me, and the longer I sat in my rocker, the more I began to think about running.

Finally, and last of all, Dr. Webb was called into the house and I cringed at the thought of dangling from a rope. I was beginning to see no other path for me. Nothing but doom filled my thoughts. How was it possible that a young man could end up being hung when all he was trying to do was live? My skin shivered and crawled,

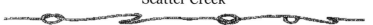

for my worst fears were assailing me. Where could I run, where could I hide, and would anyone even let me get near a saddled horse?

Looking around I knew the answer, there was no saddled horse, and the stage driver was watering his stock. I would not be allowed an avenue of escape. That driver still had us covered with a shotgun. He wasn't going to let anyone to leave without the judge's say so, especially me.

When Dr. Webb came out he looked over at me and said, "Your turn, Duke."

I must have given him a forlorn look when I turned my head because he walked over to me and said, "Just tell the truth, Duke, nothing but the truth. That's what we're all doing. If there was any kind of lying, it was from Van Cleve and Bubba Starr. That judge is no dummy. He'll be able to tell if they lied, just like he'll be able to tell if you're lying. Tell the truth, make certain it is the truth and you'll be fine."

I stood up and began my slow walk toward the front door. When I got there I had the feeling I had arrived too soon, yet how do you hold up when a judge is expecting you at said moment? You don't. Reaching for the door I opened it and stepped in. My eyes had to adjust to the dim light. I could hardly see, and then I spotted him. He was sitting at a corner table with his secretary beside him.

"Come on in, Duke. I have a few questions for you."

I slowly shuffled my way toward him.

"Have a seat. You're not on trial, this is just a hearing to determine if there needs to be one."

I sat across from him and noted what seemed to be written statements lying on the table in front of him.

These were now official documents, although I didn't know it at the time.

"Duke, I have six sworn statements here including Dr. Webb which says that the sheriff drew first. Now, I have to say from a law standpoint, I find that hard to believe, but there seems to be some evidence to support their statements. The other two statements say that you shot first while Captain Starr's back was to you. I want you to tell me in your own words what happened, and there is no room for error on your part. I need the truth, because if you lie to me, I'll have you placed in irons to face trial for the murder of a sheriff."

I swallowed hard and looked at his wife for support. "I was coming down from the barn loft when I heard horses ride into the yard. They were facing the house when I came out the barn door. Captain Starr said he wanted to arrest me, and asked where I was. I spoke up from behind and said, "I'm right here.

"He whirled his horse around and dragged iron while he was doing it. I didn't have any choice but to defend myself."

"I see." His wife was writing everything I said, and it was then I noticed the statements were in her handwriting, but signed by the party in question.

"I didn't wait to see if he could hit a standing target, I stepped to the right and shucked my own pistol. I had the added benefit of being on solid ground, while his horse was dancing this way and that every time he pulled the trigger."

"This isn't your first feud with Captain Starr."

"No sir, I've had a few run-ins with him and Bubba. They've been trying to do me in for a few years now. Captain Starr killed my pa."

"How do you know that?"

"Pa told me himself just before he died."

The judge didn't say anything for the longest time while deep in thought, and then he looked at me and said, "Duke, your friends are the only reason you're not getting locked up right now. Their stories are the same as your own. I know about you shooting Bubba, I know about the first shooting with Captain Starr. I also know that the former Greene County Sheriff Morris Wright has been killed as well. It seems to me that you've been caught up on terrible trouble which was no doing of your own, but let me tell you this. If I ever find you standing before me in a court of law, if you ever get into trouble again, I don't care what for, I'm going to throw the book at you and I'm going to lock you away for the longest time allowable under the law. Do you understand me?"

"Yes sir." I trembled.

"Now, get out of here before I change my mind."

I got up from my chair and walked out the door, expecting at any moment for the judge to change his mind, but he didn't. I opened the door and stepped out onto the front porch with my freedom. I wanted to shout halleluiah right there, but I held my tongue, not knowing what the judge's reaction might be.

Going to the corral I began to saddle my horse. John Stone and Vern walked over to me and John asked, "Where are you headed, Duke?"

"I'm going to find the rest of my family. This war is over for me. I promised Pa I would find my sisters."

"I think one of your sisters is staying at the Larkin home in Gainesville. Now, as for the other," he offered, "you know where all of them are."

"Thanks John, I'll always remember the riding we did together. Same for you Vern," I said while I saddled Jericho. When I was finished I put a halter on the US horse I'd been riding from time to time, but the judge appeared on the front porch and put a halt to my plans.

"That's US Government property, Duke. You'll have to leave that horse here."

I didn't argue with the man, but my friends gave him a few queer looks as he stepped into the corral and looked the animal over for himself. I finished cinching my girth tight and led Jericho out to the front porch steps. Here I gathered my rifle and slid it into the scabbard on my saddle. I rolled my brother's rifle up into my blanket roll and tied it behind. This made stepping into the saddle more difficult, but I was able to get around it.

Before I actually mounted, I walked into the house and said goodbye to Captain Bowlin, the man who had been my mentor for the last few years. I fought back tears, but I think he understood. To me he had been a better instructor than my own father. Not to put down my father at all, but Nathaniel Bowlin knew how to teach his ideas to a new generation of young folks, something Dad had found difficult.

"You take care of yourself, Duke," he said.

"I will, sir."

"You were one of my best men, and yet you were just a young man. You can do anything you want now. So go build a dream," he said.

"Thank you, sir, and well, you can build your dreams too."

"Maybe, but do me a favor. When it seems like the whole world is stacked against you just remember you're the best there is and if you can't make it happen, no one can."

"I'll do that, sir."

We shook hands and I went outside, saying goodbye to the men I'd ridden with. When I was finished, I shook hands with Judge Isaac Parker.

"Keep your nose clean, Duke."

"You won't be seeing me in front of you, sir."

"I pray not."

Stepping into the saddle, I waved goodbye and headed down the road to Gainesville. Now I know that to be the same place Bubba and Van Cleve had headed, but I wasn't afraid of either one of them or the two together. I had them pegged. They were cowards. They had run for cover when the bullets started flying and neither of them wanted to face a gun.

I also knew the sheriff would be laid out at the coffin store of J. Nutt. Likely Morris Wright would be there as well. What I had to do was swing wide to the west and come in from that direction in order to avoid running into enemies. All I wanted was to talk with my sister if she was at the Larkin home. I knew it was on the west end toward Scatter Creek.

I rode to the house and just as I stepped down from my horse, Bubba Starr came around the house with his gun drawn. I didn't wait to see what he wanted. He had a gun pointed at me, so I shucked mine and started toward him as I squeezed the trigger. One, two, three times I

squeezed my trigger and I saw him go down. He squirmed on the ground for a moment and then his body relaxed. He was dead.

Mrs. Larkin appeared at the front door in time to see me standing over him, and I have to tell you, it was time for Duke John Robinson to run! She screamed and I looked up to see my own sister standing behind her. I had to run, but I couldn't. I wanted to talk with my sister.

I heard wagon wheels coming up behind me and the sound of horses on the road. I turned to see Judge Isaac Parker pile out of his coach and start my direction. As he neared, I handed my gun to him and swallowed hard, for I knew what was coming. He had just told me.

"What are you handing me that for?" he said looking down at Bubba.

"Sir, you said..."

"I know what I said, and I know what I just saw. You were acting in self-defense. I was over at the J. Nutt coffin store when I saw this shooting. Take a look," he said pointing toward the store. "I was able to see everything from where I stood. There's no need for another investigation. It was a clean shooting. Now, put your gun away."

"Yes sir."

"What are those ashes over there, son?"

"That's what is left of the courthouse, sir."

"Looks like this case is going to be a nightmare. Is there a place to stay here in town?"

"Yes sir. There's the jailhouse." And that's how I first met Judge Isaac Parker.

He stayed on to sort out the mishap and I learned a good deal from him when it came to settling human

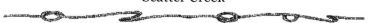

affairs where the law was concerned. First he examined all of the bodies, then called in available witnesses and had each of them make a statement. Then he sorted through the statements in order to develop a proper time line of events which had taken place leading up to the shootout. I never saw somebody dissect information like him, because when he was through, he knew more about what had happened than I did.

"Let this be a lesson to you, Duke. Always stay on the side of the law. With the war over there's going to be all types of lawlessness on both sides. Stay clear of trouble and you'll be fine," Parker advised.

"Now son, I don't see any wrong doing on your part. You were defending yourself, but it does look an awful lot like you were seeking revenge." He stopped long enough to let that sink in and then proceeded. "If I thought you baited him for revenge, I'd hang you, but I don't see any real evidence, only suspicious circumstances. Do you see what I mean?"

"Yes sir, I know it looks suspicious, but I wasn't looking for trouble. Bubba Starr dragged iron, didn't say a word."

"He drew and you beat him. Son, this country is going to need a few deputies to sort matters like these out. I'd like you to consider becoming one."

"Can I have some time to think about it?

"If you change your mind, I'll be at Davidsonville for the next few months. Wright's wife and brother-in-law have skipped town with thirty thousand dollars in county funds, money Wright himself had embezzled. If you run into them out west, you be sure and wire me where they are."

"Yes sir, I surely will."

"I know you're young, but I sure could use a good hand like you, Duke. If things don't work out like you plan, look me up."

"Yes sir, I'll do that."

"Just remember what I said, if I find you in front of me for any reason, I'll throw the book at you and I don't forget names or faces."

I swallowed hard and shook my head. I knew the judge meant business, but I wanted to go west and see what things were like before I settled into a job where everybody was shooting at me like some kind of shooting gallery.

I stayed in town along with Judge Parker to see that everything was wrapped up and he was satisfied. At the same time I managed to locate my sisters. They had been living right there in town. I visited until things were wrapped up and then I saddled up to head west.

I rode west with the stage. Judge Isaac Parker had commandeered the US brand horse I'd been using, making it his own personal stock. I guess he liked the looks of it.

At Fort Smith I looked things over and thought to myself that the judge was going to be king in these parts. Now I didn't know much back then about how life could play tricks on a man, but I was learning and I should have taken the job he offered me right then, but that's one of those things a young man has to learn the hard way.

Before leaving town I met a young man named Ian Durant who told me of a plot of land in Indian territory, and all I had to do was file on the water rights for the three water holes in the area and the grazing rights and

three hundred square miles would be mine. That got me thinking. I had deeds in my possession when I rode for Peace Valley. I even had Judge Isaac Parker's John Henry on them.

I crossed the river at Chaffee Crossing by raft for two bits and headed for my new home. I was headed west. I had a good portion of my money and I now owned water rights to all that land. It was then I began to whistle an old tune, *Peace in the Valley.* I was coming home.

JohnTWayne.com

Special thanks: To the Greene County Historical Society, and the Randolph County Museum in Pocahontas, Arkansas.

The Kansas City, Fort Scott and Memphis railroad later became the Rock Island Line. The St. Louis and Iron Mountain railroad was their competition. The two railroads met at Parmalay in 1883 and the town of Paragould was officially born. Although the sight had been surveyed in 1882 it took another year for the town to really begin construction. For the most part it was a survey revealing wooded lots and swampland. Trees would have to be cleared and removed if there was ever to be a meaningful town here.

Jay Gould was one of the most powerful men in the United States at the time. He controlled thousands of miles of railroad across the United States which included a five thousand mile monopoly in the southwest. James Paramore was of similar stature and the two tycoons merged in Paragould.

When building a railroad, there were often mile long strings of red tape which came with the endeavor. It took real men to push such projects through to completion, men who would not sit and wait on a permit or the issuance of one. Their stance was; if a state was that slow, they would finish the project and pay the fines.

When building the railroads, the men would use the wood from the trees they felled in order to make the ties. This meant they had to have their own mobile sawmill. As the portable sawmill moved through the forest, so did the railroad. This prevented the builders from having to import railroad ties from long distances.

The men would clear a path of nearly twenty feet on either side of the tracks as they moved through the forest cutting a swath nearly fifty feet wide. This allowed for a barrier if a tree fell, so no trees would land on the tracks themselves.

Men building the railroads in Arkansas were family oriented men who needed work. They worked from light to dark in mosquito infested swamps in order to push the line through. They often left home long before sunup and returned long after dark, but they did manage to sleep in their own bed late at night.

The vast forests in Northeast Arkansas were judged to have been one of the few remaining hard wood forests left in the nation. "It was nothing short of a timber man's paradise, trees in every direction as far as the eye could see," the late Jim Hayes stated.

Judge John O'Steen ran one of the mercantile's in Gainesville. Later he moved to Paragould and became the mayor.

Captain Nathaniel Bowlin was one of the most colorful characters of the time. He was ruler of Bowlin's Island, an island in the St. Francis River that's named for him. The captain was from Missouri but had southern sympathies. He was a crafty horseman, sly as a fox and an expert marksman. During the war he organized his own military outfit, and relentlessly harassed the Federal troops in Missouri. He was never commissioned by the Confederate States of America as a Confederate. He claimed the name of Swamp Fox and the name was justified. He spent the entire war effort proving too crafty for the Federals to catch.

He was eventually given a commission by Merriwether "Jeff" Thompson, but that commission was to conduct maneuvers as an independent bushwhacker, something Bowlin was very good at. Perhaps this suited Bowlin best. He wanted to conduct the war on his own terms, and not answer to any hierarchy or anyone else.

More than once when he learned of Yankees in Southeast Missouri he would organize a group of men, strike the Yankee's while they had their guard down and disappear into the swamps of northeast Arkansas.

De'Laplaine was established between Cash River and Black river. De'Laplaine was the first trading post established by the French in Northeast Arkansas area and is rich in farm culture today.

Here are seven men who died fighting for the rights of all Americans to remain free upon the land. They lost, yet they are no less the hero. It is becoming quite evident 150 years after the fact these men were fighting for state sovereignty and the right of a state to not have to bow down to the Federal Government. While the north won the war, every northern state lost their sovereignty as well. In essence, everybody lost! I am dedicating this book to these brave men who knew what Federal Over-reach was 150 years ago and fought so hard against it.

Pvt. Josiah S. House 47th TN Infantry Co. F
Capt. Samuel KP House 12th TN Infantry Co. F
Pvt. William W. House 12th TN Infantry Co. F
Lt. Jones R. T. 47th TN Infantry Co. H
William Henry Watson 12th TN Infantry Co. F
Steven F. Crider 10th KY Calvary Co. C
Thomas H. Langley 19th TN Calvary Co. C

Other books form John T. Wayne include:

Catfish John
The Treasure of Del Diablo
Ol' Slantface
Blood Once Spilled
Cowboy Up! (a book of quotes)
Captain Grimes (Unreconstructed) *Part One*

CPSIA information can be obtained
at www.ICGtesting.com
Printed in the USA
FFOW03n2333200318
45721536-46570FF